RECIPES FOR REVENGE

A FOUR-COURSE NOVEL

G. M. Barlean

Less Traveled Roads
Publishing

Less Traveled Roads Publishing
http://lesstraveledroads.wordpress.com

ISBN-13: 978-1479115969
ISBN-10: 1479115967

Cover art by C.K. Volnek
Edited by Carol Weber

DEDICATION

I would like to dedicate this book to the chef who taught a culinary class I once took.

You were an ass.

From all bad things something good may come. You, sir, inspired this book.

On a more upbeat note, I want to thank Victorine Lieske for beta reading, Carol Weber for editing, and C.K. Volnek for creating the cover design.

**Other works by
G M Barlean**

Casting Stones, New Unabridged Edition
(Including three stories of the Casting Stones
Series – **Prelude, Casting Stones** the novel, and
Conclusions)

Prelude
A short story and introduction to the Casting
Stones Series

Casting Stones
The Novel

Conclusions
A short story, which brings closure to the Casting
Stones series.

All four books are available on Amazon.com as e-
books. **Casting Stones, New Unabridged Edition**
is also available in print.

Coming soon:

Dead Blow
Suspense

FIRST COURSE

A SPICY STARTER

SAUSAGE- STUFFED JALAPEÑOS

1 lb. bulk pork sausage
1 teaspoon ground cumin
½ white onion, minced
8 ounces cream cheese, softened
1 cup Parmesan cheese
Cheddar-Jack blend cheese
Fresh cilantro
22 large jalapeno peppers, cut in half lengthwise
and seeded

Cook sausage in skillet with onion and cumin.
Combine cream cheese and Parmesan in bowl and
add drained sausage mixture. Put 1 Tablespoon of
mixture into each pepper half. Sprinkle with
Cheddar/Jack. Bake in 9 x 13 greased pan at 425
degrees for 15 to 20 minutes. Garnish with fresh
cilantro leaves. Serve warm.

GLORIA DAVIS

Gloria Davis held out the silver tray of glasses filled with sparkling champagne. Mrs. Rothwell gingerly selected a glass from the tray, took a sip, then grimaced and put the glass back on the tray. "Sparkling water," is all she said to Gloria Davis. She didn't as much as make eye contact when she gave her command. Larry, Gloria's boss, was quick to add, "I told her to buy the best. So sorry." Larry shot Gloria a nasty look.

He most certainly did not tell her any such thing.

He didn't know the first thing about planning a gathering for Bentley and LaSalle. Gloria had spent hours preparing the guest list, sending invitations to the "right people," booking the room, ordering flowers, hiring caterers and bar service...the list went on and on. Not once did Larry as much as look at any of the plans she presented him. Ass. The buck never stopped with Larry Holmquest.

"So sorry, Mrs. Rothwell." Gloria offered, but the champagne-snubbing woman turned her back. The help was dismissed.

On her way to find Mrs. Rothwell a Perrier, Gloria Davis could feel her face burn. To the outside world, she tried to keep a placid exterior, like a calm sea. But underneath her quiet surface, at least lately, dark waters churned. She stopped to look at herself in a large ornate mirror on the wall of the upscale loft apartment. Peering around the enormous floral bouquet, she examined her reflection. Pushing up her glasses, she adjusted the tortoise shell barrette holding back her light brown hair. *Calm down, Gloria.* She wondered if she should have worn the new blue cardigan she'd bought, instead of the tan one she felt so comfortable in. They say royal blue is a power color. *No*, she thought to herself as she smoothed the top of her buttoned sweater. Tan is safe. Standing out in the crowd wasn't Gloria Davis' style, after all. Yet, being treated like the help was really ticking her off. But what could she do?

Larry Holmquest, Acquisitions Director and her boss at Bentley and La Salle Investments, counted on her to do all of her work *and* most of his as well. She organized this cocktail party for the new client they landed last month – the key word being *they*. Clients with the name and money of Hugh and Belinda Rothwell could help keep the investment firm running smoothly for a long time. She was proud to have been a big part of creating the portfolio that won the Rothwells over in the end.

Although Gloria had been with Bentley and La Salle for ten years now, she had only worked under Larry for the past year and she'd come to hate the job. He made her doubt her abilities daily and she didn't know if she could stomach staying at B & L much longer.

Normally, she swallowed hard and didn't let things bother her. Gloria Davis was no complainer.

But when she thought about all the countless hours she had spent going over reports and projections with both Belinda and Hugh...and Larry just sat there in his expensive suit and polished shoes, pretending he had done all the work. He never gave her any credit or even as much as a thank you. It was a sticky pill to swallow. Why should she keep working so hard for someone who didn't appreciate her?

Still, although Gloria was quite skilled at cussing Larry out in her mind, when it came to a face-to-face confrontation, well...it was just easier to grin and bear it. The things she would have liked to tell Larry Holmquest were like a volcano building at a low boil, never allowed to erupt. Yet, for tonight, she had little choice but to do her job and do it well, regardless of the anger burning in her heart for Larry Holmquest.

Once in the kitchen, she took the top off a green glass bottle and poured it in a champagne glass. Larry popped his head in the kitchen.

"You got that drink for Belinda?" He saw it in her hands and hurried over to take it. "I'll take it to her. By the way, the jalapeño appetizers are getting low and we could use refills on champagne. Hop to it."

He made that horrible noise inside his cheek that sounded like he was encouraging a pony to run. He gave her a condescending wink, then whisked the drink away.

Outside the kitchen door she heard him say, "Belinda, my dear, I personally got your drink for you."

"Sorry your help isn't on the ball this evening," Gloria heard Mrs. Rothwell say. "You know what they say about good help." Then Gloria heard them laughing with smug superiority.

As she began to put the new batch of jalapeños on the baking sheet, she tried to ignore their self-righteous laughter ringing in her ears. But the more she thought about Larry's attitude and Belinda's elitist comments, the angrier she became. Truth was, for tonight at least, part of her job *was* to refill bowls of mixed nuts, keep ice buckets fresh, wipe up spills, and pick up napkins left sitting for "the help" to throw away. She hated the thought, but that was exactly who she was tonight. *The help.* Nevertheless, she was more than just a great party host. She was also the Assistant to Acquisitions for Bentley and La Salle. Not that anyone here cared. Tonight, she would only be known for her sausage and cheese stuffed peppers, which were disappearing just about as quickly as she put them out.

She took the new batch of jalapeños out of the oven and put them on a serving tray. Just as she was about to take them out into the party, a striking man walked into the kitchen and took her by surprise.

"Well, hello there," he said, with a pleasant smile and a smooth British accent.

Gloria's mouth dropped open a bit. She'd seen her share of handsome fellows. She was thirty-five. She'd been around the block when it came to men.

Well. No. Not really.

She had only dated a couple of men over the last ten years and neither of them had worked out so well. Sure, she'd *seen* a handsome man or two. Sure, she'd even found herself alone in a room with one. But none had ever seemed quite as tasty as the one in front of her now.

"My dear. Are you the lovely person concocting these wonderful morsels of spiciness everyone is enjoying so much?" He approached slowly, his eyes entrancing her and his voice, smooth as butter, putting her under his spell.

Her face flushed. Gloria stuttered and looked down at the jalapeños on the tray. "Well, yes…I-I…it's nothing, really."

"Nothing? I think not. It's very much *something*. Aren't you that bright young protégé I've heard about? The assistant to acquisitions, isn't that right? There are murmurings about your talent, my dear." His hand reached out to sneak a jalapeño from the tray.

Manicured nails. Gold cufflinks. No wedding ring. Her vision glazed over and she looked up into his dark brown melty eyes.

"You heard someone say that? Who? Mr. Holmquest?" She could hardly believe such a thing. Larry never gave her any compliments. How could he squeeze them in, after all, what with being completely preoccupied with himself?

"No, no, dear. Someone else. Not that dreadful boss of yours. Horrid man, truly. Now, back to you. Not only have I heard how intelligent you are, but also, you are clearly a gifted chef, an amazing hostess, as well as a beautiful woman." He leaned on the counter and gazed at her, smiling a wickedly charming smile.

Her face grew so hot it felt as though she'd burst into flames. Heavens, it had gotten warm in the room. She fanned herself as she gazed at him. "No, no. Not me. Don't be silly," she could barely speak above a whisper. He was teasing her. She didn't know what to say. She wasn't often teased.

"I am most certainly not silly. You *are* special. I can tell." He wandered over to the champagne bottle and filled his glass. "You put this party on, did you not? Well it's fabulous. One of the best I've been to in a very long time. You did a magnificent job. The food is wonderful, the setting upscale, the crowd perfectly selected."

At that moment it occurred to Gloria she *had* carefully selected every person in attendance – yet she didn't know who *this* person was.

"I'm sorry, I don't believe I caught your name." Gloria felt a twinge of panic. Had this con man wandered in uninvited? The safety of her wealthy and important guests could be in question at this very moment as she drooled over the handsome cad standing before her!

"Very good, Ms. Davis. Suspicious, as you should be." He nodded in approval as he reached into the inner pocket of his expensive suit jacket and brought out a business card. "Damon F. Hade, at your service." He bowed ever so slightly, never taking his eyes from hers.

Heat rose to her face again as she leaned forward to examine the card. She touched it with her finger. Even the paper felt warm to her. She had to get control of her libido and think straight.

"I'm with Hugh and Belinda. We should have let you know I was coming. Hugh mentioned it to Larry, but he possibly forgot to tell you?" Damon left the question hang and she nodded her head, not surprised Larry would forget.

"What are you to the Rothwells?" She asked, still concerned, but also hoping he was on the up-and-up as he was indeed the most captivating man she'd ever met.

"Yes, yes, of course. You are good, aren't you? I'm Mr. Rothwell's personal assistant. I do, very much, what you do for Mr. Holmquest." He smiled.

"Oh, I'm not Larry's personal assistant..." she started to explain but looked down at the hot pads on her hands and reminded herself she'd be taking

Larry's suit to the cleaners in the morning. She was not only his brains, but also his brawn. She flushed red with embarrassment as her fists clenched inside the hot pads. How had the job she started in ten years ago actually managed to become less important? Larry Holmquest, that's how.

"May I be honest with you?" Damon asked, his voice filled with concern. "I overheard the way Larry treated you when Belinda had her little 'I'll only drink Dom' moment. She treated you like you were just the help or something. You didn't like that, did you?" He paused. "Or at least, you shouldn't have liked that. I know I wouldn't have."

Gloria blushed. Was she that transparent? She took off her mitts and picked up the tray of jalapeños. She shouldn't be having such a personal conversation with one of Mr. Rothwell's staff, even if he was a smoldering hotty from the UK. She owed more discretion than that to the company that gave her a paycheck. Besides, she couldn't afford to say anything negative about her boss; she needed her job. But boy, would she have liked to pour out her problems, and Damon seemed *so* willing to listen.

"I understand. You really can't talk about it. Well, I'll tell you what. I want you to know I think you're marvelous. Maybe you should go talk shop with Larry's boss. Maybe he'll realize you're the brains behind his buffoonery. I believe I've only heard Larry tell crude jokes and talk about sports so far this evening. Show them what you're made of, Gloria." Then he snuck one more jalapeño, popped it in his mouth, and left the kitchen.

Gone as quickly as he arrived. Like a dream.

She contemplated for a moment and then decided Damon made a good point after all. Maybe she *would* take the opportunity to let people know she was more than just a good cook.

Gloria exited through the swinging door of the kitchen and went into the great room to put her jalapeños on the buffet. People mingled and chatted, their glasses in well-manicured hands…both women and men. It was a typical Bentley and LaSalle cocktail party. Plenty of top shelf liquor and pretty women, mixed with wealthy power-mongers. What a world. Now, why did she want to keep this job again?

Larry Holmquest stood on the steps leading up to the second level, asking for everyone's attention. *Great. A speech.* He did love the spotlight. He smoothed back his hair and hitched up the waist of his trousers.

"Can I have your attention, please?" Larry's voice boomed above the hum of the crowd. Like the perfect employee and party hostess, Gloria went over to turn down the music while Larry spoke. "Thank you, thank you," he began and the crowd quieted.

There was very little Gloria liked about Larry Holmquest. Although good looking by many women's standards, he was not her idea of handsome. That big chin, the blow-dried hair styled up like a big German lifeguard from Baywatch, those big, perfectly straight teeth…and those dimples. Gag. He was a Ken without a Barbie and he looked just as plastic. Then Gloria clapped her hand over her mouth to cover her giggle as she thought about how she used to strip off her Ken doll's pants when she was little, and how surprised she was to find a genital-free, smooth front. Now she couldn't help but see Larry that way. Then Gloria heard Larry say something that caught her ear.

"At this time, I want to thank someone very special for all of the hard work they did to help persuade Hugh and Belinda to sign with B & L."

Gloria smiled as she tilted her head and waited with grateful eyes for Mr. Holmquest to finally give her the credit she deserved for all of her hard work. She toiled many long hours and really needed some affirmation for her extra efforts.

"Without this person, there would be no way I could have pulled together the one thing that won Belinda and Hugh's confidence. The information I received from this source was top-notch and, without it, I know the Rothwells would never have agreed to allow us to handle their investments." He paused and searched the room. His eyes landed on Gloria. She stepped forward hesitantly just as Larry said, "Doug Frieze, get up here, you dog!"

Behind her, Gloria heard a man begin to laugh as he made his way to the front of the room. Larry boomed between guffaws, "Good old Doug not only told me about the great new restaurant out in the Knolls, but also gave me some of my best jokes, and everyone knows, it's food, booze and laughs that always land the client!"

The fools in the audience cackled and laughed at Larry's predictable sense of humor, and Doug stood beside Larry on the steps, pumping his fists in the air as though he'd just won the Olympics. Gloria almost sneered with disgust, but then hid her emotions. She would never be "one of the boys." The way they acted, she didn't really want to be. She turned to leave, but from behind she heard Larry say, "Gloria…did you think I forgot about you?"

Larry's words stopped her cold as they echoed across the room. She turned slowly, her smile returning. Could it be? Had her time finally come? Her eyes shined bright with hope of getting recognition for the role she played in convincing the Rothwells to invest with B & L.

"Don't forget to fetch some more of those jalapeño poppers. Hey everyone, a round of applause for Gloria! She's a pretty good cook and not a bad little secretary, too!"

She heard a few laughs, coughs, and disinterested claps. Gloria felt the room begin to spin. Embarrassment rushed from the tip of her toes up to the top of her head and her blood boiled. She wanted to scream. She wanted to rant and shout. But Larry had already moved into the crowd and was slapping backs and grinning like a fool, so proud of his ridiculous oration.

Her feet mechanically carried her into the kitchen. Everything spun around her in a blur. She was numb. Completely numb. "Secretary?" She cringed as she said the words aloud. She had worked hard to gain a title at a prestigious firm. "A pretty good cook?" She put her fists on her hips, her knuckles turning white. She single-handedly arranged this entire celebration.

"Not what you were hoping for, I would venture to guess." From behind her, Damon's words, stating the obvious, were filled with empathy.

She shook her head as heat flushed her face and she felt overwhelmingly consumed with the fire of anger. She was so furious she didn't even hear Damon walk up behind her, then peer around into her face now stained with sizzling tears of rage.

"You really can't let him treat you that way. You warrant better. He doesn't deserve you at all, you know."

The words rang truer than any she'd ever heard. She began to pace. Who in the hell did Larry Holmquest think he was, anyway? He practically announced to the room she not only had no part in landing the Rothwell account, but also took away the title she'd earned, and announced her to be no more than the girl who made the stinking jalapeño poppers. She slammed her hands flat on the counter, and then held herself steady as she fought her sobs.

"Oh, Gloria. Don't cry. Crying isn't going to help you. I promise you that." Damon's voice floated like a fog around her dizzy head and she could feel herself giving in to his underlying suggestions. He convinced her. He was right. She couldn't be soft all of the time. She had to toughen up.

Gloria had ignored, tolerated, and turned the other cheek long enough. Forgiveness and feeling sorry for herself obviously wasn't working. Kindness had gotten her nowhere and her hours of overtime and hard work only made *Larry* look better.

But what could she do – become a lazy employee? No. Not only was it not in her nature, but it would likely get her fired. She had to do something, though. She had to, if nothing else, speak her mind...set things straight. Gloria needed to demand the respect she was owed.

Her tears dried up, but she realized her breathing now came in pants. Holy hell, it was hot in the kitchen. She stripped off her tan cardigan and jerked the safe little barrette out, letting her hair fall down loose around her face.

"There's the spirit. I see where you're going with this. You're going to go out there and give him what for, aren't you?" Damon nodded and encouraged her with a broad smile.

Gloria stared at him and wondered where this man had been all her life. He was so in tune with her needs.

"Damn straight I am. I've had it," she told him. "No more being a door mat. It's time I stand up for myself. No one else is going to do it, after all!"

"Right, you are!" His encouragement fueled Gloria's burning desire to set Larry straight for once and for all.

She stormed over to the counter and poured herself a glass of champagne. With shaking hands she stared at the beautiful bubbles then drank it down in one huge gulp.

"There you go. That's what you need – a bit of liquid encouragement. That will help." Damon nodded and smiled.

Gloria poured another glass and drank it fast. Then a third. Damn. That was good champagne…even if it wasn't up to par for the likes of Belinda Rothwell. She set the glass down, feeling her face glisten with sweat from anger and alcohol.

"No time like the present," she said, feeling a fire in her belly she could hardly recognize. She was going to march out to Larry Holmquest and tell him how lucky he was to have a kick-butt Acquisitions Assistant like herself. "Wish me luck," she said as she stormed past Damon.

From behind, she heard his encouraging applause.

Gloria strode over to Larry Holmquest with a confidence unfamiliar to her. She pulled herself up to her full height and jutted out her chin in defiance.

Larry was flirting with Tabby Goldstein, a painfully thin woman with heavy eyeliner, bright red lipstick, and a silky gold blouse with no brassiere – not that she had much to restrain. Gloria overheard Larry tell Tabby he would love to show her the bedroom suite upstairs. Before Larry noticed Gloria standing there, the woman licked her glossy red lips as her lusty eyes glanced up and down Larry's tall form. Gloria was clearly interrupting an entirely different kind of party just waiting to happen.

"Mr. Holmquest." Gloria tried to be loud and firm, but years of quiet and polite subservience were hard to overcome in one moment of valor.

He looked at her over his shoulder, irritated, as though a pesky fly had landed there. He gave her only a glance, and then he ignored her. Slipping his arm around the current acquisition he now sought, they began to move away from Gloria as though she wasn't even there.

"Mr. Holmquest," Gloria demanded, but her voice came out whiney and shrill. "I need to talk to you," she added, trying to control her voice, but the jazz, the crowd, the distance he had already put between them…she was left standing with rebellion in her mind, failure in her heart, and a weak tone on her tongue.

She hurried after them and touched his arm. Lightly. He didn't notice. She grabbed his arm. He spun to face her.

"What do you want!" His face merely inches from hers, he hissed like a cobra sprung. She lurched back, stunned by such venom.

"Can't you see I'm busy?" His eyes narrowed and his expression told her he had no respect for her whatsoever.

Every ounce of courage drained from her like an avalanche of snow charging down a mountainside. She was left cold…ice cold. And confused. No words came. No thoughts. Just hollow fear and the need to flee.

He rolled his eyes. "Get me a fresh drink." He thrust his empty glass toward her. "And make it quick. I'm heading upstairs to land a new deal." He winked, blatant and rude.

Like a mere machine designed only to serve, she took the glass from his hand, moved, trancelike, over to the bar, and had the bartender freshen the ice, pour scotch with a splash of club soda and add a fresh wedge of lemon. Still stunned, she walked back and handed him his drink, which he took from her without as much as a thank you.

Gloria drifted back to the kitchen in a daze, defeated before her battle had even begun.

Once the doors to the kitchen closed behind her, her tears flowed freely. She scurried to her purse and dug through it to find her bottle of migraine medication. She could feel her brain beginning to swell behind her eyes and the dull thud of her heartbeat pulsating in her temples. She washed the pills down with more champagne, which she knew was a cocktail for disaster. What did it matter? She felt such a failure. Not one celebratory drink would have been held high in toast this night if it weren't for her. The prospectus that landed this client, the perfect selection of people gathered in the room, the setting, the food, she helped with or did *everything*. It was all her, yet some man with a joke got credit from her boss and she was announced to be little more than someone who answered the phone and made appetizers. The more she thought about it, the more her ego swelled, bloating her desire for revenge. Not one solitary person at this damn party would give her one iota of credit unless she demanded it.

She felt the heat of Damon's body approach before she heard his words. The drink, the medication, the emotions…all played together to make her swoon and sizzle at his nearness.

"*I* know it was you who made all this happen. *I* know you are amazing." His hot breath and perfect sentiments blew wisps of hair around her ear. She melted at the feel of his breath as she let Damon's words caress her mind. It was all she needed to fortify her resolve.

As if on a mission, she turned and went to the counter and began to prepare a new batch of jalapeños. It would be the last batch she made for the night, and then she planned to quit this God-forsaken job and move on with her life. This wasn't the only place to work in this city, and with her skills, it wouldn't take long to find something else…something better. She was above this trash.

"That's the spirit," Damon said from across the room…encouraging, supporting.

She mixed the browned sausage and onion with the cream cheese and shredded cheddar, a little cilantro, some cumin, and a dollop of sour cream. She deftly chopped up a white onion and tossed it in with the mixture, and then she heard the words that lit her soul on fire and made her imagination dance.

"I believe there is a small box of rat poison beneath the sink."

Such quiet words.

Almost a whisper.

She swallowed hard as she stared at the bowl of filling in front of her. She turned to the sink and her eyes drifted down to the door below it, slightly ajar. She saw the yellow box. She bent over and reached for it like it was an ingredient she used every day. She snapped up straight, coming to her senses.

"No. I couldn't do that." She said, her hands still itching to grab the box.

"Couldn't do what?" Damon asked.

"What you're suggesting." She returned, unable to say the words out loud.

Damon remained silent, and she began to wonder if he'd ever said anything at all. Gloria continued to stare at the muted shadow of the box lurking just inside the cupboard beneath the sink. Then the door to the kitchen swung open, allowing sounds from the world just beyond to color the dark moment with laughter, music, and clinking ice in heavy-bottomed glasses.

"Gloria. More jalapeños, and hurry up! More champagne. More ice. I thought I could count on you. What the hell are you doing in here, resting? This isn't your party. There's work to be done!"

She turned to stare open-mouthed at Larry, his tie askew, one of his shirttails hanging out, and a hint of red lipstick smudged on his chin. Her stomach churned. What a disgusting pig of a man. Has he no shame?

"Chop, chop, girl." He added, but before he could leave the room, she called out to him and he stopped, turned to her, and waited, tapping his foot impatiently.

"Mr. Holmquest." Her courage peaked. "I do not appreciate the way you're treating me. I think you should give me more credit." She couldn't believe the words even made it from her mouth. The second they hit the air she felt a mixture of relief and victory all mulled together like a deadly elixir, so bittersweet. But then she felt panic creep in. "I did the ma-ma-majority of the w-w-w-work for the Rothwell project." *Of all times to stutter.*

Larry stared at her for a second, letting her comments float like a foul smell. Then he chuckled. "Well, I'm s-s-s-sorry!" He burst out laughing at his imitation of her. "You're not serious are you?" He raised an eyebrow in disbelief. "I mean, you *do* realize the hierarchy of things, right? Me, boss…you, employee?" He said it very slowly as though she were too stupid to understand. "I mean, did you actually think I would give you the credit for landing Rothwell? Seriously? Hon, little people like you are a dime a dozen. I can find any fresh face right out of college and within three months they'd be running circles around you."

Gloria had suspected all along he didn't appreciate her, but to hear him taunt her with such cruel words left her stunned. Her throat closed up so tight she could barely swallow.

"You just get back to work. The party is still hopping and you have a lot to do. Oh, and there is a red wine spill on the white carpet so you'll need to get to that right away, and someone puked in the bathroom." He shrugged and grinned, then turned to go. He leaned back in to add one more comment. "And if you want to keep your little job, you'll lose the ego. Not only could I find someone smarter than you, but it wouldn't take much to find someone better looking."

The final cut. It went so deep. The door swung in and out…in an out…in and out…like a clock ticking away her life. She stared at the space Larry Holmquest had taken up while he essentially broke her back down to nothing.

From the corner of her eye, she saw the yellow box of poison…now sitting on the counter. She glanced at it, then at Damon. He nodded slowly. She stared at the black silhouette of the image of an overturned rat, then she picked it up and dumped no less than three large tablespoons into the mixture and stirred it until it blended nicely. Larry Holmquest deserved to be sick. Deadly sick.

"Yes, Mr. Holmquest. Let me make you a special batch of Jalapeños. Just for you, sir. Please…try one. Have another. Three? Certainly! Eat the whole plate. I know how much you love them. I aim to please, after all." She filled each jalapeno to the brim with her deadly concoction as

Damon watched from the other side of the kitchen, smiling an evil smile.

She pulled the deadly appetizers from the oven and simultaneously the kitchen door swung open. Mr. Bentley entered the room.

Gloria and Mr. Bentley had never had a close relationship like she had with Mr. La Salle. Still, she respected the man whose signature was on her paychecks and the brass sign at the entrance of her office. He was a hard worker and a decent human being from what she had observed over the years.

Gloria swallowed hard at the realization of the pan of poisoned jalapeños she held. Steam rose in the air in front of her and guilt surely emanated from her every pore. This moment of normal brought her out of the dark place her mind had taken her.

"Oh, more of those wonderful peppers!" Mr. Bentley raised his eyebrows with enthusiasm and grinned as he stepped up to the counter, his fingers reaching out to pluck up one of the deadly treats.

"No!" Gloria's voice, piercing and shrill, sliced through the molecules of air like a bolt of lightning.

Mr. Bentley's eyebrows shot up and his jaw dropped. He stepped back, retracting his hand like a child who just got his knuckles rapped by a nun.

"I'm sorry," she felt a stutter coming on. "These are j-j-just t-t-t-too hot." She inhaled deeply, trying to calm herself. "I wouldn't want you to b-b-burn yourself." *Damn it, Gloria. Get hold of yourself.*

Mr. Bentley stared at her for a moment…what seemed like an eternally, long moment. He attempted a stiff smile. "I see." He backed away more, quietly nodded his head, and turned to leave the room. Every inch of his expression and body language accused her of insanity.

How had she reached this point? She had stooped to a low even she couldn't understand. Gloria didn't know how she'd ever imagined doing such a horrible thing as poisoning her boss. What had possessed her? She set the pan of tainted appetizers down and turned to stare open-mouthed at Damon…but he was gone. She looked around the room. No one was there but her. She stepped out into the party to search for him, but again found herself alone with full responsibility for the gruesome idea she had almost carried out.

Confused, she ran back into the kitchen in shame. Her mother hadn't raised her this way. Gloria Louise Davis was not an evil person. Thank God, she'd come to her senses.

Picking up the pan of jalapeños, she stepped on the foot lever for the large silver trash canister and the lid sprang open. Into the garbage they went, landing on top of used cups, dirty napkins and sweepings from the floor. They steamed, still deadly, but appetizing to look at, even at the top of the trash heap. She let go of the spring-loaded lid with her foot and it closed with a metallic bang. An exclamation point at the end of an evil idea she'd never speak of…to anyone.

Gloria untied the apron from her waist, folded it calmly, and set it on the counter. Then she tucked in her blouse and returned the tan sweater to her shaking shoulders. She straightened her hair, clipping the barrette back in place and then buttoned the top clasp of her cardigan, and cleared her throat. She was beginning to feel in control again. Like herself…but better. Stronger. More sure of who she really was. Fortified, even. Yes. Bolstered.

Walking out into the party, Gloria let the kitchen door swing and whoosh behind her. With composure, she scrutinized the crowd, looking over the expensive cocktail dresses, glittery handbags, and costly suits and silk ties. From manicured fingernails to stiletto heals and salon tans, there wasn't much genuine about this group of people. Then her eyes landed on Larry Holmquest, the greatest counterfeit of them all. There he stood with his drink in his hand, bragging about something inane she supposed. Without hesitation, she marched over and jabbed him in the arm three times with her index finger.

He looked down at his arm, then back at her with a look that normally would have chilled her to the bone. A new confidence kept her fear not just at bay, but completely absent. She had crossed a line between sanity and surety, doubt and faith. She'd found her fiery molten center and had almost erupted, but now felt only a controlled boil. She was better than the evil she thought she would do. She was better than all of this, and she knew she was going to be fine, no matter what.

"I quit." She said. No more words were needed. No reason to embellish or explain. Her voice was steady, strong, and clear.

Larry smirked. "Yeah. Right." He glanced down at his Rolex then looked back up her with one raised eyebrow. "That time of the month?" He reeked of Scotch and arrogance.

She turned to leave. Why give him the satisfaction of the temper now building in her? But something pulled her back. What about her own satisfaction? Didn't she deserve to gratify herself this once? Gloria gave herself permission to go ahead and say what she'd dreamt of saying for so long. What the hell. Just moments ago she was planning to kill him with rat poison. The least she could do was to slice him up with a sharp tongue.

"Larry. You big. Idiotic. Horse's ass." Her voice rose, but remained steady, commanding and completely devoid of any hint of a stutter. Everyone within earshot could hear. Heads turned, conversations quieted, and ears bent to listen.

"I've had all I plan to take of you. I've fetched your coffee, taken your clothes to the cleaner, made appointments for your haircuts, manicures,

31

massages and exfoliations. I've run to purchase booze for your stash in the office so you could coast comfortably numb throughout your days. I've covered your ass when you came back from lunch too tipsy to make sense on the phone. I've sent your mother, your air-headed girlfriends, and your clients birthday cards and get-well cards and presents. I've made excuses, lied and bragged on your behalf and generally saved your sorry carcass long enough. I've done all of that, *and* half the work *you* should be doing. But I'm through."

Gloria had the room's full attention now so she faced the crowd, turning away from Larry...*the loser*. She wanted to make sure Mr. Bentley heard what she had to say.

"Larry Holmquest is a womanizing, lazy, dim-witted, underachiever who somehow made his way up the good-old-boy ladder, doing the-devil-knows-what to earn his place behind the desk in the mahogany-lined office he takes his naps in. He hasn't put together projections or marketing strategies worth a cat's crap in a litter box since the day he walked through the doors of Bentley and La Salle, and if it weren't for my hard work, connections, and brains, he wouldn't be swilling booze on the company dime right this very minute."

Mr. Bentley looked as though he might pass out, but oddly enough, Belinda and Hugh Rothwell seemed to be covering their mouths to keep from snickering.

Gloria continued, as everyone seemed riveted to her rant. "I've seen this man drooling on his desk during a two hour nap after lunch. I've solely run the office while he left for lunch at 10:45 in the morning and didn't return until 2:30 in the afternoon. I've arranged for him to play golf, go to expensive restaurants for dinner and I've booked flights to resorts where he claims he's wining and dining "clients" when I know full-well he's rendezvousing with women at the expense of Bentley and La Salle. I've watched him spend hours playing online poker and writing off a myriad of personal items to his expense account…such as that Rolex twinkling on his wrist right now."

Not once did Larry close his dropped jaw to say a solitary word. He was beyond stunned, and obviously incapable of intelligent argument. Mr. Bentley's face had turned a shade of crimson that looked unhealthy…for Larry, at least. Gloria walked toward the kitchen door with poise, and then returned her comments to Larry.

"The truth is, Larry, if Bentley and La Salle weren't footing your bill and turning a blind eye to your shell game, and if I wasn't working like a dog to keep you smelling like roses, you'd barely have a pot to piss in or a window to throw it out of."

Gloria looked over to Mr. Bentley. "Good luck," was all she said, and then she pushed through the swinging doors, picked up her purse, and left the apartment from the back. The service elevator was just fine for now. She'd find something better soon enough. She'd rise above this dip in the road. Soon she'd have a new job…a better one. And as for Larry Holmquest? He could go straight to hell as far as she was concerned. She was fairly sure he could find his own way there.

* * *

Larry heard the back door of the apartment slam. Instinctively, he turned to the crowd with his palms up and he shrugged. "Women!" He laughed and rolled his eyes.

He laughed alone. Party guests, fellow employees and his boss stared at him with straight faces and hard eyes.

"Oh, come on. Surely, none of you bought that load of bull. She obviously blew a mental gasket. The mousey little secretary went cuckoo." He made circles with his index fingers by his ears.

The room remained silent with the exception of whispered voices at the back.

Mr. Bentley took control. He went to Belinda and Hugh and led them toward the door in the foyer. Larry could hear Bentley telling them, "I'll be in touch tomorrow. And yes…of course…this situation will be rectified immediately."

"Dougy!" Larry pointed playful finger guns at Doug Frieze. "Let's get outa here…go grab a beer at The Embassy lounge." Larry tried to pretend everything was as it always was, but Doug shook his head, backed away, then turned to leave.

Larry made other weak attempts to talk to others as the crowd quickly thinned, but soon he was left facing Bentley who now stood in the center of the room, glaring at him like a man about to gun him down on the dusty streets of the old west. Mr. Bentley turned to the bartender and cocked his verbal gun with a tone of voice that meant nothing but business. "Send us a bill. We'll take care of it tomorrow. Please leave." The man behind the bar put down the bar rag and hurried to the door without a word. When Richard Bentley got serious, people listened, and the bartended obviously didn't want to get caught in the crossfire of the upcoming shootout.

Then Bentley glared at Larry, aimed and fired. "Clean out your office and get the hell out by ten tomorrow morning. Don't bother to put me down as a reference. I'd wager you won't find work in this town any time soon." Mr. Bentley's neck burned red with anger and his mustache twitched.

"Richard, you can't be serious." Larry laughed. He stepped forward and put his hand on Bentley's shoulder. Mr. Bentley looked at it with disgust, then picked it up like something diseased and flicked it from his shoulder. Larry's hand dropped to his side and he searched his mind for what he could say, but Bentley beat him to the draw.

"Don't waste your breath. You think I didn't know you were shirking your work off onto that poor girl? As long as the work was being done, I suppose I was willing to ignore your lack of ability or ambition. That was *my* mistake. But without her, you're not worth a thing to me, Larry. Nothing at all." Bentley turned to leave, but turned to add one more shot between the eyes. "Oh, and tomorrow morning, I plan to call Gloria Davis and offer her your job." Bentley smiled and reached up to smooth down the corners of his mustache. "I just thought you'd like to know." Then the older man left the room like the king of business he was – with authority and finality.

When Larry heard the door close behind Bentley, for a moment he wasn't sure what to do. One moment he had been the life of the party and the next, his secretary was reading him his last rites and nailing his coffin shut. *Bitch*. Well, he could sit down and cry about it or he could make the best of a bad situation. Larry went to the bar, picked up the bottle of expensive scotch, and took a long pull straight from the bottle. He eyed it and saw there was only a quarter of the amber liquid left. That would do. He sat down in the leather side-chair and continued to light fire to his mouth with the proof of high quality scotch. He had already been inebriated enough he would have had to call for a cab. If he finished this bottle, he'd be doing good to make it up to the bedroom to crash for the night. Still, he intended to drink every bit of the booze Bentley and LaSalle paid for, and *then* he'd take the rest of it home with him as a retirement bonus. *Stupid Gloria. Bastard Bentley. Wonder if I can still play in the company golf tournament next week?* His stomach rumbled as he finished off the bottle. Throwing it on the floor, he stumbled toward the kitchen to dig around for something to eat.

Larry almost fell when he plunged through the swinging kitchen doors. He staggered past the counters, his vision distorted as he searched for something to put in his stomach. Apparently getting fired made a man hungry. He giggled to himself, and then the room spun around him and he fell, crashing into something cylindrical and metal. He lay on the floor, reaching around with his hands, trying to blink away his drunkenness and figure out what he'd crashed into. His hand landed on something he recognized. He'd held the shape in his hand several times that night. He made himself sit up and there on the floor in front of him, his unfocused eyes saw a pile of those wonderful sausage-stuffed jalapeños.

"Jackpot!" He hollered. "Score!" He stuffed an entire pepper in his mouth, grabbed two more, and gobbled them up, practically without chewing. Before he was finished, he'd dumpster dived and eaten all but one of the garbage goodies.

He lay back on the cold tile floor, and within moments, or minutes – he couldn't track time – his belly began to churn. Something didn't feel right. It was probably the alcohol, he thought. He shouldn't have drunk so much. But then he felt something more. Something worse: a gurgle in his stomach – a cramp in his bowel. He twisted to his side so he could stand, but out of nowhere, a man's hand clamped down over his mouth and this action, for whatever reason, laid him flat and immobilized him completely.

Larry stared up with fear into the eyes of the man whose hand seemed to paralyze him.

"Hello, Larry. Pleased to meet you." The man with the British accent smiled, his words gliding like soft butter being spread on warm bread.

Larry moaned beneath the man's hand. *Who is this? Where did he come from?* Larry's mind raced, as his stomach twisted and boiled. *And why can't I move my arms or legs.*

"I'll bet you're wondering who I am…what I'm doing here. Right?" His calm smile emitted an unearthly feel.

"Well, let's just say I, too, am in acquisitions. Kind of like yourself. Of course, I'm far better at it than you. I do my own homework, Larry. I don't rely on others to do it for me. That's a good way to get burned…but of course you know that now, don't you Larry?"

Larry's eyes were wide with alarm. The longer the man's hand pressed into his face, the hotter the hand became…burning hot.

"Getting a little warm in here for you, Larry?" The man chuckled. "Ha. Well, you know what they say. If you can't take the heat, get out of the kitchen." He chuckled, pleased with his word play. "Trust me, Larry, old boy, this is like a cool breeze compared to where you're headed." He looked around. "Ah, I see you did a little dumpster diving. Hard to resist those spicy jalapeño stuffed peppers, huh? Even if they were loaded with rat poison."

Larry's brain attempted to process what was happening. He tried to scream, but it came out as a muffled cry beneath the palm of the man's hand.

"Just no accounting for taste, is there." He reached over and popped the last jalapeño from the floor into his mouth. "Tastes fine to me. Go figure. Well, I'm used to the heat I suppose. Say, let me give you my card." The man pulled the rat poison from under the sink and put it in Larry's hand, then reached into his breast pocket and pulled out his business card. He held it in front of Larry's eyes and although Larry's vision was blurred with the burning fever of panic, by the time he finished reading the words, everything became quite clear.

The card read:

Damon F. Hade
Acquisitions

Then the letters turned blood red and Larry's eyes filled with terror.

DEMON FROM HELL
Acquisition of Souls

The letters, inked with blood, drained off the white card and dripped down onto Larry's face. Damon began to laugh as he left the room, and the last thing Larry saw before the poison began to bubble from his lips and he gasped his final breath was Damon's pointed red tail as it swished out the back door.

SECOND COURSE

SEPTIC SALAD

4TH OF JULY POTATO SALAD

5 lb red potatoes, unpeeled, boiled, cooled and
refrigerated overnight, then cut up into cubes.
1 medium red onion, diced
1 lb bacon, fried (or baked), crumbled.
1 small package (approximately 1 ½ cups) cherry
tomatoes, halved
3 large stalks of celery, diced

Dressing:
1 cup salad dressing
1 cup mayonnaise
¼ cup white vinegar or pickle juice
¼ cup white sugar
¼ cup milk, cream or evaporated milk
1½ teaspoon salt
1 tablespoon mustard, whatever variety you like
¼ teaspoon pepper

Prepare all ingredients for salad and refrigerate
overnight. They should be firm and cold when you
mix them up. Make the dressing. Put all ingredients
in the bowl, add the dressing and stir together.
Refrigerate. Never leave potato salad out for more
than an hour unless sitting in a bowl of ice to keep
it cool. Refrigerate immediately after serving.

ROBERTA BUTLER

Keeping Secrets

Fortunately there wasn't much Roberta could remember about that day in the garage so many years ago. Uncle Lester only had Roberta along for some kind of sick, on-the-job training.

"Bobbi…Danielle, how 'bout let's go for a walk?" Danielle was seven at the time, Roberta only four. They walked to her father's workshop out behind the barn. Lester suggested they play hide and seek. "You count, Bobbi." He shut her in the small room at the back of the garage so she wouldn't peek.

She didn't know what happened after that. All Roberta really remembered was the single light bulb hanging in the middle of the ceiling, the smell of motor oil, and the sound of her cousin, Danielle, whimpering. Roberta tried to peek out from under the door, but all she could see were feet, and she didn't like kneeling on the dirty floor.

When Uncle Lester finally let her out of the little room, he smiled and messed up her hair. She'd been a good counter. Danielle stood behind him. She had red eyes and blotchy cheeks.

"What's wrong Danielle? Were you crying?" Roberta walked over to reach for her cousin's hand, but Danielle jerked away and turned her back on

Roberta. Lester was holding tight to Danielle's hand, keeping her behind him.

"She got into some of your father's things and hurt herself." Lester said, staring deep into Roberta's eyes. "Don't tell on her, though. She'd get in trouble. You don't want to get her in trouble, do you?" Lester's face was stern, the way grown-ups look when you've done something wrong.

Roberta shook her head. She was a good girl. She tried to obey – especially the aunts and uncles. Mamma said she should be 'spectful.

"Isn't that right, Danielle?" Lester didn't take his eyes off Roberta. He held Danielle's hand, but Danielle didn't say a word.

Lester leaned down and tickled Roberta. She shied away. She didn't like him, but she didn't really know why. Something was happening she couldn't understand. Then they walked back to the house. Uncle Lester pulled a candy from his pocket. Butterscotch.

Roberta still gagged at the smell of butterscotch.

* * *

Roberta hung up the phone. She put her head against the wall of her apartment, thinking about the conversation she'd just had with her mother. The family picnic was coming up, her mother told her. That meant Roberta would have to see Lester.

Damn the annual family picnic and the ugly memories it brought with it.

As she brushed her teeth before getting ready for bed, she considered how many hours she had spent over the years thinking about what Lester had done to Danielle that day in the garage. None of it made any sense then, but now...now she knew. She brushed her hair and stared at herself in the vanity mirror. She should have done something to help. But what? She was just a little girl doing what she was told to do. She didn't understand what was happening. Maybe she thought if she just kept being a good girl, it would be different. After all, the grownups seemed to think it was okay for Uncle Lester to take them out alone.

This was the only time Roberta remembered being with Danielle when "it" happened. Roberta had even forgotten the incident until she was a little older. They were kids. Danielle crying that day didn't seem so odd. Someone was always crying about something. Things never seemed fair to kids. It was just one more time a grown up did something she didn't understand. She was too young even to know what questions to ask or what things to tell. Besides. It didn't happen to Roberta. It happened to Danielle. The memory wasn't as strong. So life moved on for her in spite of bad uncles and secrets little girls had to keep.

But life didn't fare so well for Danielle.

Did Uncle Lester continue to "take Danielle on walks"? Roberta didn't know. She only knew from that point on, she herself avoided this uncle. When Roberta got a little older, he asked her to go on walks, but she shook her head, no, and clung to her mother's legs. But Danielle became a sullen little girl whose face grimaced in anger all the time. Danielle didn't want to play with the other kids anymore. Roberta remembered overhearing her mother talking on the phone about how Danielle failed classes…got caught smoking…and was promiscuous. The adults talked about Danielle being a "problem child." And then the family had no other choice but to face how serious the problem was.

Roberta remembered sitting at her mother's table when the awful phone call came.

"Oh, hey Dotty." Roberta's mother was peeling potatoes at the sink as she cradled the telephone in the crook of her neck.

"What's wrong?" Roberta heard the shift in her mother's voice. "Who called you?" Her mother sounded panicked. "No." Roberta heard the potato peeler hit the metal of the sink. Her mother gasped.

"I'll be right there." Her mother's voice shook and Roberta saw shiny tears spill over the bottom rim of her eyes. She rubbed them away with the back of her hand.

Danielle, at seventeen, had committed suicide.

And there, but by the grace of God, go I.

* * *

Now Roberta lay in bed trying to sleep. She'd be having nothing but sleepless nights right up until that damn family picnic. Her mother knew how she felt about going, and she knew exactly why she didn't want to be there, too.

Roberta thought back to the year she was thirteen. It was right before a family picnic. Everyone had gathered at her mother's house.

Roberta tossed in bed as she tried to push back the ugly memory.

Lester had his eye on her all that day and she felt unsettled and dirty from his stares. Roberta had been avoiding Lester since that day in her father's garage. Usually he ignored her, but this day his eyes were filled with an angry glare as they followed her everywhere she went. Each time she was within proximity of him, she could feel his eyes burning into her.

She winced at the feeling her memory brought. A shiver ran up her spine as she envisioned him when he caught her alone in the hallway.

"Don't you have a kiss for your Uncle Lester?" He sneered and grabbed her upper arms, pulling her to him.

She didn't have time to consider an answer or escape before he kissed her on the mouth, hard, thrusting his tongue in through her lips. It happened faster than a scream could crawl up her throat. What was he doing? Her mind struggled to understand. She pulled away, broke free, fell back a step or two. Roberta brought her hand to her mouth to wipe away the spit, then she scrubbed at her lips, hoping to erase the assault. Her eyes were filled with disbelief, but his were consumed with disgust.

Roberta buried her head in her pillow, wishing she didn't have to have this ugly seed planted in her brain.

"Is that how your boyfriends do it?" He had snarled, his upper lip pulling into a jealous sneer. Then he huffed, and with one last leer, turned to stalk away. She heard him mumble, "Little slut."

She ran to the bathroom and tried to collect herself. She thought she should be crying, but tears didn't come. She didn't understand what had happened, why he was so angry, or why he hated her so much. She shook with fear, feeling alone and guilty somehow.

Roberta got out of bed and went to the bathroom, hoping a glass of water would help her shake the past from her brain.

She leaned on the sink and rested her head against the mirror, closing her eyes and accepting the memories that washed over her. After a moment, she pulled her head back and stared at her reflection in the mirror. Funny how back then she felt so alone even when so many family members were so near. But no one ever saw what Lester did. He made sure of that.

When Lester and his wife, Camilla, left that year, Roberta sat in her room trying to work up enough courage to tell her mother what had happened.

She could hardly breathe, thinking about the right words to say. She went to the kitchen to talk to her mother who was up to her elbows in soapsuds as she did dishes in the sink.

"Uncle Lester kissed me." Roberta hadn't meant to blurt it out like that, but she had no idea where else to begin.

Her mother looked at Roberta with a vacant stare, then refocused her attention on the dishes as though Roberta had never said a word.

"Of course he kissed you. He's your Uncle. You hug and kiss all your aunts and uncles." Her mother scrubbed harder on the pot and it banged against the steel sides of the sink.

Roberta paused for a moment, staring at her mother's hands working on the stubborn pot. She took a deep breath. The tears were about to come. She had to make her mother understand.

"No. He kissed me…like a boyfriend." She could hardly say it. "With tongue." She gagged at the thought then, and gagged now as she went over it again in her mind. "And I think maybe he's done stuff like that to Danielle too."

Roberta waited. By mentioning Danielle, her mother had to take her seriously. She could vividly remember her mother scrubbing harder, soap bubbles and water splashing up the sides of the sink, her face turning red and her back stiffening, but still, she did not respond. Roberta waited. Minutes passed. Finally, she asked, "Mom?"

Her mother spun around and met Roberta's questioning look with accusing eyes filled with denial. "Don't you ever say those filthy words again. You hear me? Uncle Lester would never do that. Your Aunt Camilla wouldn't allow it. That's a horrible thing to say about good people." Tears welled up in her mother's eyes…tears for Lester and Camilla it seemed. Then she turned her back on her daughter and resumed washing dishes, leaving Roberta to deal with the issue alone.

So alone.

Roberta shook her head at the memory, left the bathroom and went back to bed. How could her mother have done that? She clutched at her stomach, sick from the past that refused to stay shoved to the back of her brain.

That day, after she had told her mother, Roberta wandered away from the kitchen in confusion. She ran outside to hide in the barn where she cried tears she thought would never stop. When she was done, she felt ashamed, embarrassed, and guilty. But she had made her decision. She would never say another word about Uncle Lester. She knew where she stood when tattling on grown ups. Alone. She had apparently let her mother down. Been a bad girl. Done something wrong and surely deserved God's punishment, although she didn't know exactly what she had done. She didn't care.

Whether Lester had moved on to other cousins, neighbor kids, or innocent children at church, Roberta didn't know. Whatever he'd done to Danielle had been enough to ruin her short life, though. By the time Danielle was in high school it was fairly obvious she didn't care if she lived or died. And then she must have decided dying was the easiest, because she took her own life. No note. No blame assigned. Just a young girl on the floor in a pink bedroom, two wrists slashed open and blood soaking into the fibers of the tan carpet beneath her.

What he did to Danielle and what he would have done to her if he had the chance was more than Roberta could bear. Roberta never shared her ugly memories and always suffered alone. It made her sick. Her guilt for not figuring out how to help Danielle was becoming more than she could cope with. When Danielle took her own life, Lester's secret became Roberta's biggest regret.

Family Picnic

Regardless of her dread, Roberta drove up to the park. Under the picnic shelter was her family, all gathered for the damned family picnic. What a joke. She trudged through the grass toward the day she dreaded. At least for this picnic...she had a plan.

"Well hey there, Bobbi." Of course. Lester had to be the first person to greet her. He slithered up and stood in front of her, halting her in her tracks. He pulled up his high-waisted pants and adjusted his thick black-rimmed glasses.

"Bring some of that tasty potato salad of yours?" He winked as he rubbed his hands together like a rat. "Maybe you brought some special just for me." Then he laughed that laugh – that breathy, nasal, disgusting laugh. She shivered and bile rose at the back of her throat.

His crooked yellow teeth made every hair on her arms stand on end and it was all she could do to stare past and ignore him. Roberta never had much luck finding her voice around Uncle Lester. For all the blustering and chest beating she did about him when she was alone...in front of him, she was still the little girl filled with guilt and secrets too ugly to tell.

Yes indeedy, Uncle Lester, you filthy bastard. I brought you special potato salad alright, she thought. In her imagination, she'd roundhouse kick him, launching him backward into the long picnic table filled with assorted family favorites. The frog eye salad would fly through the air, splattering Cousin Carl, and the beanie weanie would summersault high, then land on Aunt Helen's beehive hairdo. Roberta would soar like a ninja through the rafters of the picnic shelter, landing atop lecherous Lester. *And now you will pay, you pasty-lipped pervert!* Nasty, tainted, potato-salad-filled-Tupperware in her arms, she would scoop out the poisonous portions by the handful, shoving it into Lester's mouth and forcing him to swallow. *Swallow, you son of a bitch.* Lester would wrench from side to side, but Roberta would be stronger, her super strength coming from years of repression, guilt, and rage.

What a delightful imagination she had.

The sound of children screaming snapped Roberta back into the sad moment of reality she really existed in – standing at a frigging family picnic, once again dealing with Uncle Ugly. It was like a nightmare she couldn't wake up from. Roberta wanted the old bastard to die, preferably in front of her. She would never forget her guilt until she saw his ugly face go flaccid and lifeless, and know he'd never hurt another child.

For her sake…for other little girls…and mostly for Danielle, Roberta intended to make things right. Today was the day.

She would kill Uncle Lester.

Before this moment, she hadn't been sure if she could go through with her plan to eliminate from the world this pustule of a human being. Nevertheless, as the picnic approached, she contemplated the years of countless bottles of antacids, nightmares, and sleepless nights...and she planned. Her plans led to one solution. The only solution Roberta could imagine.

He had to die.

Roberta dug through her cooler to get the container of un-tainted potato salad. She set it out on the red checked tablecloth of the long picnic table. She wasn't entirely sure how she would feed Lester the plate of revenge she had planned, but where there was a will... Roberta had left the small container of Lester's *special salad* in the cooler, and was about to go back to shut the lid and grab a soda when she saw Aunt Camilla, Uncle Lester's wife, across the picnic shelter. Roberta hated Camilla by extension. Why would Camilla marry such a putrid man? How could she not have known what a monster he was? And why was Roberta's mother unable to see Camilla for who she was? The way Roberta's mother defended her sister and brother-in-law rubbed salt into Roberta's deep wounds.

Three children came running up, shaking Roberta out of her thoughts and into the present. "Push us on the swings," they squealed and pulled at her hands. Roberta let them drag her toward the swing set just yards away from the picnic shelter.

As she pushed the children on the swings, she glared at her family under the picnic shelter. There they all were, eating their picnic fare from plastic plates and guzzling tea and lemonade. Why were they all so happy? Didn't they know a child molester sat among them? How could they not see he was, if nothing else, a disgusting human being? Did they not notice how he never visited with the other men? What normal grown man spends most of his time alone, with the women, or around children?

Roberta's young cousin Stacy ran past on her way to the shelter. Roberta watched as the girl of eight or so ran close to Uncle Lester…like Icarus flying too close to the sun. Lester's hand sprang out and grasped the young girl's arm, pulling her into a hug. Roberta held her breath as she watched in horror. It was as though she was watching a movie of herself or Danielle as a child. He picked Stacy up and sat her on his knee. Roberta could imagine the teasing questions he asked as he bounced his knee. Roberta began to walk with determined steps toward them, only to see her mother hurry over, take the young girl by the hand, and lead her away. Roberta then saw Camilla, also standing at the ready with watchful eyes.

Had the summer of Roberta's thirteenth year made a difference after all?

Roberta sat down on a bench by the swings, more determined than ever to go through with her plan. The children had run off to play on the slide and so she took a moment to figure out how she would serve Lester his own heaping plate of retribution. It was time.

Roberta stood and walked to her cooler with resolute steps. She picked up a plate and put a couple pieces of fried chicken on it, then casually, she lifted the small container of potato salad from her cooler and put it all on the plate. She stared at it. She'd crushed up an entire bottle of her insulin pills and mixed the powder in with the salad. She didn't mind sharing her pills at all.

She was actually going to do this. Her chest heaved as her breath quickened. She glanced around as she buried the now empty plastic container deep in her cooler. No one was watching that she could see. She turned and saw Lester, sitting alone…staring at her. He licked his lips and smiled. It didn't surprise her. He always made it easy to hate him.

"Lester. I made a plate for you." She set the heaped plate in front of him and sat across from him to watch him eat. She wanted to make sure he took every last bite.

"Well, I thought you'd come around eventually." Lester said as he picked up a fork and plunged it into the heap of salad. He shoved it into his mouth and then chewed with his mouth open. "You know. I've always liked you, Roberta. You probably didn't even know it. I'll bet you even

forgot how close we were when you were little."
He smiled and shoveled in another bite.

"Oh, I remember quite well, Uncle Lester."
Roberta glared at him as he continued to scoop in
the yellow mayonnaise-coated potatoes. "I
remember you and me and Danielle taking a walk,
then playing hide and seek in my dad's garage."
The words tasted foul in her mouth.

Lester grinned as the fork hovered above his
plate. "Yes. Danielle liked those secret games. You
would have too. Little girls love…games." He
stared at her, searching her eyes for a reaction.

"You think so, Uncle Lester? You think little
girls like your games?" Roberta couldn't hold back
any more. Her voice shook, but she had to confront
him. She couldn't cower in fear of this beast any
longer. "Because you know, I don't think Danielle
liked that game at all. I think she thought it was
wrong." She swallowed hard. "And when I got
older, I figured it out. You are a sick child
molester, Uncle Lester." She said it. The words had
come out. "And I think you're the reason Danielle
killed herself." Roberta glared at him, waiting for
his response. Her whole body shook with anger and
her neck burned with blood vessels ready to burst.
She could hear the sound of her heart beating in her
ears and could have ripped him apart with her bare
hands in that moment.

"Oh now, Bobbi. That's just silly. I never did
anything Danielle didn't want me to do. She was
my special girl. That's all."

He just kept smiling. He'd eaten all of the potato salad and now his fingers were covered in grease as he devoured chicken, sucking at the bones. He waved a cleaned bone in front of himself.

"Young girls need a good male figure their lives, and I was happy to oblige." He laughed a little as he sucked clean another chicken bone.

And then he coughed.

A strange look came over Lester's face. He looked to be attempting to cough again, but no air came out.

Roberta smiled. He was choking.

"Something wrong, Lester?" Her heart skipped a beat and evil joy filled her body. "Something not right, old man?" Lester's eyes bulged even more from his obnoxious face. It looked as though he wanted to mouth words, but he only held tight to the table. Roberta looked around. No one was paying any attention to them. Children scampered past, old women sat across the shelter reminiscing about old times, and the rest were out in the open area playing Frisbee. She was going to get away with this.

Then something in her clicked. Shifted. Like a veil being pulled away from her brain allowing her to see clearly. Chills ran up her spine and every hair on her arms stood on end. She couldn't sit and watch someone die, especially at her own hand. Not even Lester. Dear God. What had she become?

Roberta was about to jump to her feet to drag him to her car and speed away to the hospital, when Camilla came up behind her husband. Roberta stared at her aunt with wide eyes haunted with her own guilt. She had to do something and quick.

Then Lester tried to stand, but Camilla put her hands on her husband's shoulders and pushed him back down.

"No, Lester. You rest. It looks like you're not feeling well. Just sit tight. I'm sure it will pass." She glared down at Lester, then gazed up at Roberta and offered her a strained smiled.

Roberta didn't know what to do or say. She watched Lester begin to struggle. "I think he needs help. Something's wrong. I..."Roberta began to confess, but Camilla stopped her.

"Hush, Dear. Don't say anything." Camilla raised her eyebrows and gave Roberta a stern look. "There's nothing wrong with Lester. If he's struggling, well, he probably deserves to be, doesn't he?"

There was something in her eyes – something cold and knowing. Roberta covered her gasp when Lester reached up his shaking hands and grabbed onto his wife's wrists, but Camilla just pushed down on his shoulders with more force.

Roberta's mother came up to Camilla. She glanced down at Lester, then up to Camilla. "Everything okay?" She asked quietly as she scanned the crowd with watchful eyes. She gave

Roberta a strained smile and shook her head. Roberta read her mother's eyes, which told her to stay quiet, sit still, don't say a word.

"Just fine. I think Roberta could use a little help, though." Camilla continued to pin Lester to his seat. She had to use quite a bit of her strength.

"Now calm down," She told him as she leaned down and murmured in his ear, breathing heavily. Her eyes held Roberta's as she talked to Lester.

"Just be still. This is our special little game. Don't tell anyone. It's our secret. Ok."

He jerked and kicked a little as he sweated and turned gray. She continued to hold him down with all of her strength being used now.

"It won't take long. Just be quiet. Shh. Don't make noise. There. Almost done."

The words she said in Lester's ears dripped with sarcasm and shook Roberta to her core. These were surely words he'd whispered in Danielle's ear so many years ago. Camilla knew. This was Camilla's revenge…not Roberta's.

And then his struggling ceased.

Roberta sat in dumbfounded silence as Lester began to slump over into his plate. Camilla pulled him up with one arm around his chest and one hand under his chin. She smiled and acted as though she was hugging her husband. Then Roberta saw her pinch him. Lester didn't react. Camilla took his wrist and felt for a pulse. She shook her head at Roberta's mother.

"Roberta," her mother's words startled her. Roberta turned away from the shocking scene in front of her. Her mom was standing beside her. She searched her mother's eyes in panic. "Don't say a word, Roberta. Just hush. We'll take care of this." Roberta's mother had one hand on Roberta's back and the other gently stroked Roberta's hand. Then her mother turned back to Camilla who nodded at her sister. Roberta's mother added, "Just go along with what we do. Ok?" Roberta nodded her assent, her mouth hanging open, her brain racing to understand what was happening.

Then Camilla hollered out. "Help! Something's wrong with Lester!"

She lowered his carcass back onto the cement of the picnic shelter and Roberta's mother led Roberta by the hand as they hurried over to Camilla's side.

Uncle Jack came running to help. "Oh, dear. Did he pass out?" Jack knelt and put his ear to Lester's mouth. "I don't feel any breath." Jack opened Lester's mouth and looked in. "I can't see any obstruction." He hoisted Lester up and began to perform the Heimlich maneuver. Roberta watched as Camilla and her mother attempted to look worried.

Camilla knelt beside her husband. "I have no idea what happened. One minute we were laughing and joking and the next minute he was unconscious."

Jack began chest thrusts to no avail. Whispers floated through the family members who had gathered around.

"Sis?" Camilla looked up for Roberta's mother. Roberta's mother knelt down, the rest of the family forming a circle around Camilla, Jack and Lester. "Do you know what happened?" Camilla asked Roberta's mother.

"No. I was talking to Roberta and suddenly you were calling for help. Jack? What's going on?" Roberta's mother wrapped her arm around Camilla's shoulder in comfort. Jack shook his head and shrugged.

Roberta couldn't believe what was happening…the way her mother and aunt seemed to have this all under control. How could they know what she had planned? Roberta looked around the small crowd and saw people's faces. Oddly enough, expressions were less concerned than one would expect.

Roberta's eyes landed on Cousin Debby. Did Lester take you on walks, too? What about Cousin Cora? The more Roberta searched around the family's faces the more she wondered how many other little girls lost their innocence to Uncle Lester's sick games…how many other family members hadn't watched their children closely enough.

Then Camilla slapped Lester's face. Lester gave no reaction. She slapped him again. Still nothing.

"Camilla, I don't think that's going to help." Jack reached out to put his hand on Camilla's shoulder, but she pulled away and slapped Lester once more. "Camilla!" Jack shouted.

Roberta's mother stood and pulled Camilla up and away as Jack pounded on Lester's chest and blew into his blue lips.

Sirens grew louder as they approached. Someone had called 911, but Lester wouldn't be saved. Camilla paced and mumbled to herself, Roberta's mother by her side. Roberta couldn't understand the surreal scene playing out before her eyes.

The rescue squad ran up and began to work on Lester. They started with quick movements, attempting to resuscitate. Then their motions seemed to slow as they pumped air into his lungs. Finally, they loaded him onto the stretcher and carried him away. Camilla and Jack went along and the remaining family stayed back, murmuring in disbelief, but not so much in disappointment, or so it seemed to Roberta.

After things quieted down, Roberta went to her mother. She stood staring at the woman, waiting for an explanation, afraid to speak of the horror she'd just witnessed…the horror she was a part of.

"Camilla caught him with one of their grandchildren." Roberta's mother couldn't look

Roberta in the eye. "When Camilla told me, I told her about what you'd said all those years ago." Tears welled up in her eyes. "We figured it was why Danielle…" She couldn't say the words. "How many girls, we don't know. He deserved worse." She finally looked at Roberta. She was shaking.

"Yes, he did." Roberta agreed with a small voice. She hugged her mother and they shared tears of fear and relief.

"How?" Roberta asked, wondering if she too, should confess.

"I don't know and I don't want to know. Camilla did something. She didn't tell me, but I saw her put something in his tea right before you gave him a plate of food. He gulped it down fast. Greedy bastard." Her mother shook her head and put her finger in front of her lips. Roberta nodded. *Not to worry, Mom. I won't say a word.*

Family members packed up their casseroles and plates and threw away the Styrofoam cups and plastic forks. At first, they were all silent and in shock. But before everyone left, a quiet laugh could be heard here and there. It wouldn't take long for this family to get over the loss of Uncle Lester. Maybe they knew more than Roberta thought. Or, maybe, they were just very good at looking away when things got ugly.

ENTRÉE

DINNER TO DIE FOR

KILLER CHILI

1 tablespoon oil
1 lb ground pork
1 lb ground beef
1 large yellow onion
4 cloves garlic
½ teaspoon red pepper flakes
(less if you don't like heat)
1 tablespoon chili powder
(less if you don't like heat)
1 teaspoon cumin
1 tablespoon smoked paprika
1 teaspoon salt
2 tablespoon flour

Bacon Molasses

Brown meats, add onions and garlic in oil. Add all seasonings to this point. Sprinkle the 2 tablespoons flour over browned meat and spices; stir until it thickens.

Now add:
1 teaspoon Worcestershire
1 tablespoon brown sugar
1- 15 ounce can Mrs. Grimes chili beans in sauce
1 -15 ounce can La Preferida Mexican
Homestyle Beans
1-15 ounce can tomatoes
1-8 ounce can beef consommé

Stir well and let simmer for an hour or longer on low heat. Stir occasionally. Serve with a dollop of sour cream and a sprinkle of cheddar cheese.

CHICKY TORRES

This Cowboy Walks Into a Bar

For the first time that night, Chicky stopped to take a moment to scan the room and see who was actually there. She propped her fists on her hips and peered through the smoke-filled room. Darn! Five women at table eight – two of whom had already had far too much to drink, and three others who looked like they wished they could go home. *Those gals will tip like an atheist at a revival meeting.* A few regulars were stacking up beer cans on two pulled-together tables at the outskirts of the dance floor. Some scruffy-looking characters lurked in the shadows back by the pool table. And then, of course, the karaoke crowd sat at the tables near the dance floor, flipping through the binders to find that perfect song they would attempt to sing.

"I need a whisky sour, two Bud Lights, and a Lone Star draw," she hollered above the steady hum of the crowd to the bartender as she grabbed a few napkins for table four.

A man bumped into her right as the bartender set the sour on her tray. "Whoa there Pard, slow down," she shot the fella a look over her shoulder. Another cowboy. Go figure. They were as plentiful as gnats at a wine bottle here in Tom Green County – especially at The GiddyUp. He gave her a wink and tipped his hat, "Sorry, Ma'am." His low voice and quick smile caught her off guard and left her speechless. He chuckled, pleased with himself, as he sauntered away with an "I still got it" strut. Oh, he still had it all right. In fact, it looked like he may have invented it.

The bartender's voice brought her attention back to her job.

"Two lights, a sour, and a draw. There ya go," the bartender darted a straw into the sour, grabbed a maraschino cherry from the little tub, dipped it in the sour, then popped it in his mouth. The tall young man pushed his long, unruly bangs out of his eyes and gave her a wink.

She was a firm 5 foot 9 inches, but she still had to look up at this gangly fellow. "Scooby, you're gonna get in trouble for that one of these days." She smiled and tucked her red hair behind her ear, making her silver earrings jingle.

"Like this bar could live without me or you." He waved her off as he headed to the other end of the bar with long, slow steps to the waiting customers bellied up there. He was right. Then off she went, shoving her way through people on her way to deliver drinks, take orders, and live the American dream, waiting tables in a Texas bar called The GiddyUp.

Chicky wasn't paying much attention to the guy she was waiting on. Letting her mind wander while she worked got her through a lot of hours waiting on rowdy crowds. Honestly, she was thinking about the last three guys she had dated. Boring. Every one of them. Oh, they were solid, decent men. They all had normal jobs and were clean and well behaved. Too well behaved. And in the bedroom? Yawn. So, she really wasn't paying much attention to the guy she was waiting on at all – at least not until his calloused fingers made contact with her hand. Some kind of chemical reaction – some kind of electricity – ran up her arm at the touch of his rough fingers, which demanded her complete consideration.

Her green eyes rose to meet his steely blues. It was the guy who had bumped into her up at the bar earlier. A bead of sweat trickled down the center of her back and pooled above her belt line. It was deep summer in Texas and even in air conditioning, it was easy to break a sweat. Chicky couldn't put her finger on why his touch woke up her senses and put a hitch in her heart beat, but the muscle in her chest certainly thumped a new rhythm when he gave her a smile. It thumped hard. It was a moment in time like so many others. It was just one more instance when one more cowboy ordered a beer and tipped her with a lusty look. But one vibe this cowboy didn't put off was boring. No. This guy looked like a good time just waiting to happen.

"So, what can I get *you*?" she asked him. His eyes sparkled and his smile widened into an ornery twist. She answered his smile with one of her own.

"You can get me some ear plugs." He winced at the woman butchering Patsy Kline at the karaoke

70

mike. His voice was low and slow and all kinds of sexy. He stood up, and with bowed legs and Wranglers hugging his adorable behind, he sauntered up to the man behind the DJ equipment. Soon the fella she already thought of as The Sexy Cowboy was at the mike.

Chicky knew the tune well. She'd met Willie at The Hall in Gruene back in 2010. When The Sexy Cowboy started to sing "Mamas, Don't Let Your Babies..." her knees gave way and her arms went limp at the sound. *Lord, help me*, she thought, as she swiped her hair away from her face. *Damn. I said I'd never date a customer again.* But Chicky Torres wasn't much for rules, not even her own.

* * *

The next morning, she woke up with one helluva hangover, and The Sexy Cowboy in bed beside her. She stared at him while he slept and chastised herself for falling into the sack with him so quickly. Nevertheless, there she was, and from what she could remember of the night before, she wasn't regretting it as much as she should have been.

Boone whined at the side of her bed. She realized she'd forgotten to feed the big black lab who normally lay on the side of the mattress the cowboy now occupied. "Oh, Boone. I'm sorry." She hurried to get up, threw on her robe, and hustled to the dog dish. Boone followed, his tail swishing side to side in anticipation. She scratched the scruff of his neck as he ate. Poor fella. So

71

patient and loyal. He forgave her every time she messed up. She glanced back to the bedroom. She sure did mess up a lot.

About a half hour later, the long, tall cowboy ambled into her farmhouse kitchen. His wranglers hung loose and unzipped on his narrow hips and his bare chest reminded her why she messed up in the first place. He stretched and yawned, then grabbed the cowboy hat he'd left on the counter the night before.

"Not ready for the day 'til the lid is on the jar," he said through the yawn as he tipped the hat onto his head. Chicky's heart thumped hard again.

"So, what is up with that name of yours, girl?" he asked her as he slid a chair up to the little metal Formica table.

She got up to get him a cup of coffee. "You take cream?" She asked. He shook his head, no. "Named after *mi Abuela Chiquita*." She smiled at the thought of the little round grandmother she loved so much.

"Nice accent," he commented.

"Half Irish, half Hispanic," she smiled with pride.

Chicky's mother was a kind loving woman, originally from Mexico. She talked to her on the phone at four every afternoon. Chicky's father was a mean wife-beating Irish ass whom she hadn't seen since she was ten. Good riddance. She was glad he left and she let his name go with him. Torres was fine by her.

She watched the cowboy as he drank his coffee. The morning sun only made this guy look better. Cooper Wolfe was his name, and that's about all she knew about him. She'd already taken to calling him Coop. "Want some eggs, Coop?"

"Naw. I don't eat eggs unless I can put chili on 'em." He shrugged. "I know. Weird habit."

Chicky's eyes lit up. "Well. You are a man after my own heart then. I just happen to be the three-time champion of the San Angelo Chili Cook-off! And, lucky man that you are, I happen to have some leftover chili in the fridge right now."

Cooper smiled. "Then bring on the eggs smothered in chili and cheese, please!"

Temper, Temper

Three weeks had gone by and so far, so good.

Chicky and Coop never got much farther than her bedroom or the bar, but she didn't mind. Everything about this guy warmed up her insides like a pot of her killer chili. His smile, his low voice, the way his cowboy hat shaded his eyes, and especially those snug Wranglers she stumbled over every morning on her way to the bathroom.

She was no beginner in the bedroom, but this guy took a romp in the sack to a whole new level. She'd been smitten, she'd been warm for a form, but never before had she fallen this hard or this fast for a man. His touch lit her on fire and just a hint of his hot breath on her neck melted her like butter on cornbread. It was no wonder she was willing to overlook a few of his bad habits.

Most of his habits weren't so terrible. One that bugged her was how he refused to close the door to the bathroom when he peed. She knew he urinated, but she really didn't need examples. Some things were private and that was one of them as far as she was concerned. He also sucked his teeth after eating and the sound scurried up her spine like a spider. But she understood it was just an old habit, and a harmless one at that. When he did either of these things she just stared into his blue eyes and remembered the night before and all his irritating quirks were forgiven.

Chicky thought about her father. He was

nothing but a bad habit. Chicky's father had stayed in their lives just long enough for her to remember the beatings he gave her mother. She remembered watching from the crack of her bedroom door as he slapped, choked, or punched her, depending on his mood. She remembered running out to stop him and her father's big hands pushing her away like a mere irritation. When he was tired of knocking his wife around, he'd slam the door and drive away…leaving Chicky to take care of her poor mother.

"Mi Chiquita, don't look at me." Her mother would say, ashamed of her bruises, and ashamed she couldn't stand up to the man she married.

Her mother stayed in the marriage because she couldn't support herself and her daughter…or at least that's what Chicky surmised. The worst part of him beating her and then leaving was that he kept coming back with pathetic apologies her mother always accepted.

It was a blessing when he finally stormed out the door one night and never returned. He didn't leave them with much, but Chicky did keep one thing. She kept a pledge in her heart that she would never, *ever* allow a man to hit her the way her father had hit her mother.

Back to Coop. The truth was, passion like theirs led to strong opinions, and strong opinions could lead to tension. Although they meshed well in the bedroom, they didn't talk that much once they left the sheets. When they did talk, she was surprised to see how few things they agreed on. Kids, politics, religion, money, goals...how could the devilishly handsome, suave, hunk of cowboy, be such a polar opposite of her every tenet?

"Oh, for crying out loud. You cannot be serious. You voted for that idiot?" She said it too loudly...too sarcastically. Even as the words left her mouth, she could see he didn't cotton to teasing. He was immediately insulted. And in another instant, he was mad. Red-faced, tight-fisted, pissed off with a capital P mad.

She could see Coop's every muscle clench. The look on his face told her even his sphincter clamped shut. He came off the couch like a horse spurred in the ribs, shot her a smoldering look meant to set her on fire, then stormed away.

"Coop?" She got up, and then hesitated. She called after him, "I'm sorry. Coop?" She went after him.

When she caught up, he spun around to face her. The look in his eyes stopped her cold. He shoved his finger in her face and barked, "You don't talk to me like that. Ever! You will show me respect, damn it!" His voice was loud, cold, and shaking with rage.

Chicky stepped back, nice and slow. That finger in her face looked awfully familiar to her. It looked just like the finger her Daddy shoved in her

Mamma's face right before shit hit the fan. The color left her cheeks and she could feel it drain down her neck. Was that her Daddy she just saw in Coop's eyes? But fear wasn't what she felt. It was something very different. Every memory of the ugly violence she witnessed as a child surfaced. Heat built up in her and repainted her face a livid red. She felt the fury tingle on her skin and her breath came in hot, quivering, heavy breaths. *Not me, buddy. Never me.*

She wasn't one for violence. Heck, she couldn't even swat a fly without saying, "sorry." She didn't know exactly what she would do if the situation arose, but she had a feeling she'd go completely Tasmanian Devil on a guy who tried to hit her. Of course, that remained to be seen.

She could see he recognized her eyes to be filled with rage instead of fear. He lowered his hand, and shoved it deep into his pocket.

"I'm sorry…I shouldn't have yelled. I just want you to love me as I am. I don't like being judged." His lowered voice and quiet words caught her off guard. She was surprised how quickly she cooled down and forgave him. It only took another moment before he had her back on the couch. By the end of a tender hour of intense love making, she had completely forgotten the entire episode.

Until his temper bubbled up to the surface again at the breakfast table two days later.

There he sat, his chest and feet bare, in only

his jeans and his cowboy hat, just the way she liked him. She picked up the hat from his head and messed his blonde hair. He snaked his arm around her narrow hips and nuzzled his scruffy cheek against her flat stomach. She set a hot cup of coffee in front of him. "Here ya go." Her voice smiled. He lifted the cup to his lips and slurped up the scalding brew.

Coop lurched from his chair, knocked her backward, and spilled hot coffee on the table and onto his lap. "What are you trying to do to me? That coffee is hotter than hell!"

Chicky caught her balance. She stared at him, surprised at his reaction, but then made the mistake of laughing. She covered her mouth, knowing she shouldn't have, but his eyes were so big and wild over such a small incident. It just struck her funny.

"Oh, you think this is funny?" Coop snarled and then hurled the cup across the room. It slammed into the wall, just six inches from her, denting the drywall, breaking the cup and splattering coffee along the way. "You like seeing me scald myself? You think that's something to laugh at?" The veins on his neck bulged out and he was screaming mad. Zero to sixty in no time flat.

Chicky stood very still as she watched him, his chest heaving with raging breaths. His fists clenched tight and instantaneous hate darkened his eyes. Chicky knew she was witnessing the actions of a man who had no control over his temper. A man who wouldn't be able to stop himself from hitting her if she said or did the wrong thing, even if it was as simple as serving him hot coffee. Her father had acted exactly the same way.

She swallowed hard. It didn't matter how much she liked this guy. He was going to have to go.

Then he did just what she figured he would. The pattern was ridiculously predictable. He turned on a dime. Just like Daddy used to do.

"I'm sorry, Chicky. I don't know what in the hell got into me." He hurried over, grabbed some paper towels, and started cleaning up his mess.

She didn't move.

"It won't happen again." The pieces of the cup clinked as he dumped them into the trash bin. "You have to forgive me."

She kept her face expressionless. She knew she couldn't give him a reason to be upset. She'd seen this play out many times with her mother and father...him apologizing, her refusing to accept his apology, then him flying back into his rage. No. She wouldn't allow it to happen to her.

Coop walked over to her and brushed her cheek with his hand. His eyes pleaded with hers. "Please. You have to say it's ok." She didn't say a word. He interpreted her silence as forgiveness.

Self-absorbed ass.

"You know you can't stay mad at me," he said

and then he kissed her and wrapped her in his arms. She put her arms around him, too. She would play nice for this moment, but locks were about to be changed and this asshole wouldn't be seeing the light from her bedroom window ever again.

Karaoke Gone Wrong

Luckily, Coop hadn't moved in with her. Chicky thanked her lone star for that blessing. She suspected he was a drifter. He hadn't told her much about himself. Before she saw his true colors, she thought maybe she could change his mind and convince him to stay put in Tom Green County. Now, she was hopeful he would ride off into the sunset, and soon. He was staying at the El Pueblito in San Angelo. He told her he worked for the Double Mesa Ranch as a temporary hand. They were branding at the Double Mesa, so at least that would keep him busy and he wouldn't be lying around on her couch for the next few days.

Good. She needed time alone to think.

Chicky lived down the road from the old Ghost Town of Ben Ficklin, Texas. Tom Green County had treated her well, right from the first week she moved into her little two-story farmhouse. Big Dan Tanner lived a mile down the road. He helped her move her crappy old furniture and was always ready to give her old pickup a jump when she needed it. Seemed every time she looked out the window, there was Dan, fixing a hinge on her garage door, or hammering a nail into a piece of siding that had gone loose. The man couldn't seem to help himself when it came to looking after her. He also gave her a good steady job at The GiddyUp, and his friendship meant more to her than any friend she'd ever had. If there was one thing she could count on, it was the loyalty of Big Dan Tanner.

"You comin' in to do payroll this afternoon?" Dan asked, his low voice growling over the phone. Dan was as gentle as a puppy but he looked and sounded like a Pit Bull. At least Chicky believed he was gentle…although he did get a crazy look in his eye when someone got out of hand at the bar. No one messed with Big Dan…at least, not more than once.

"The earth would open up and swallow that place whole if it weren't for me, you know." Chicky liked to tease Dan there wasn't enough money in the till to pay her what she was worth. He agreed readily. Truth was, she knew he'd pay her whatever she asked. Truth was, he would do anything for her and she knew it.

"I'd crawl in a hole myself if anything ever happened to you, Chicky," Dan said.

"Yeah, yeah. No need to sweet talk me. I'll do the darn books." Chicky laughed, but she knew he meant it. Poor man. When she first moved in, he tried so hard to convince her to go out with him. She knew he'd drop everything to be with her even now. But she had turned him down so many times he finally gave up. Big old love-sick puppy.

Before she left for work she sat to jot down a grocery list. She was planning to make a new batch of chili and she was almost out of smoked paprika and down to her last can of refried beans. As she wrote out the list, she hummed "Mamas, Don't Let Your Babies Grow Up To Be Cowboys." Dang it.

She started thinking about Coop. That grin. Those gorgeous biceps. That tight, flat stomach. Dang it, again! Maybe she judged him too harshly. *No, Chicky. Get a grip.* You *will* find a guy with all that heat, *and* a normal boiling point. She sure was getting tired of looking, though. Not many new faces showed up in these parts.

List in hand and resolve in her heart, she jumped in her car and headed to The GiddyUp. It was an average day. She drank too much coffee, and she yelled at the computer a lot, but in the end the numbers balanced and the checks were printed.

"Stay for a beer?" Dan peeked into her cubbyhole of an office. "Please?" His eyes drooped like a beagle's and he pouted out his bottom lip. She didn't usually stick around after work. Although she waited tables on occasion, for the most part she stuck to bookwork and helping with inventory…things like that. She could use a beer or three to get her mind off Coop, though. Maybe she would tell Dan about Coop's temper. *No.* She thought better of it. If Dan thought for a minute Coop might lay hands on her, he'd bust out of his shirt like the Hulk and grind Coop up for Burger Thursdays.

"I don't know, Dan. It's been a long day." Chicky sighed, but she knew he'd continue to beg and she knew she'd stay.

"Don't make me take a knee, girl. Just have a beer or two with me. I'll buy you a burger." His grin told her he knew darn well she'd stay, but he was still willing to go through the motions of begging her to stay.

"Cheeseburger. Grilled onions, too. No skimping. I'm worth it!" Chicky pushed up from her chair and joined Dan at the doorway. He put his strong arm around her shoulder and gave her a little squeeze. She looped her arm around his waist.

"Don't I know it," Dan said and they left the office as comfortable in each other's gait as an old married couple.

The karaoke crowd started coming in around eight and by then, Chicky had a few beers under her belt. They tasted so good after that greasy burger and she was truly enjoying relaxing in Dan's good company.

Right up until Coop walked in the door.

The man sure did take the oxygen out of the room…for her at least. He was all cleaned up and looking extra charming with a new white cowboy hat and a big shiny silver belt buckle. He looked around and when his eyes found her, he bee-lined to their table.

Chicky knew she had to tell him it was over between them. She had planned to call him tomorrow and talk about it over the phone. She didn't know what she would say. She was still trying to figure out that part. Unfortunately, her time to think was up. Tonight would have to be the night. But doing this in person wasn't going to be easy. Not when he made her heart hammer like rain on a tin roof. But just because she wanted him, didn't erase the fact he was bad for her. Yet, the man certainly did make her feel all ooey-gooey inside.

He greeted her with a wink and a kiss on her blushing cheek. His hand squeezed her shoulder, sending a spark of electricity down her back.

"Hey Chicky. I missed you, girl." He sat down, leaned over to her, and gave her another kiss – lingering and hot. He gazed into Chicky's eyes, his own eyes telling her exactly what he had on his mind. "Hey, Dan. Not tryin' to move in on my girl, are ya?" Coop didn't as much as look at Dan when he said it, but kept rubbing Chicky's knee under the table. Such confidence, she thought. It was not going to be easy to tell him it was over.

"Coop, I think…" she was about to say they needed to talk. No time like the present. Rip off the Band-Aid.

He interrupted her. "Dan, get me a beer, would ya."

Chicky stopped short, her mouth dangling open mid-sentence. Dan raised his eyebrows and made eye contact with Chicky.

"You need a beer?" Dan asked her.

She sighed. "Might as well." She might need more fortification for the conversation she planned to have with Coop.

Dan stood, looking dejected and a little ticked, and slowly ambled to the bar to get their drinks. Coop turned his back to the table so he could see the stage. Karaoke was only five minutes from starting and he was getting fidgety.

"Say, Coop," Chicky began, "We need to talk."

"We do? That sounds serious. Well, it'll have to wait because I'm in the mood to sing." Coop jumped up and headed over to the Karaoke man. Dan returned with their drinks.

"Everything ok here?" he asked, his eyes searching hers for just one reason to protect her.

Chicky hesitated then gave a quick nod. "Sure. Why do you ask?" She glanced over to Coop. He must have decided to be the main event for the night the way he was filling out song slips.

"Coop treatin' you ok?" Dan leaned heavily onto the table and waited, his worry hanging in the air between them.

She thought about it for a moment. "Dan, if I ever have trouble with a fella, I promise, you'll be the first person I call."

He gave her a big smile. "I'd better be." He stood up, reached over and gave her shoulder a little squeeze, then ambled off to help at the bar.

The night went on and the conversation she'd planned to have kept getting put on the back burner. Coop sang, she sang, they sang together, they danced, and the beer cans kept piling up. By the end of the night when Coop sang her favorite Willie song, she was walking crooked and slurring her words. He came back to the table after singing, took her by the hand and they slow danced to a nice young gal singing "Stand By Your Man." She didn't know if it was his hand on the small of her back or the light stubble on his chin brushing against her cheek, but right then, the last thing on her mind was ending her relationship with Cooper Wolfe. She wanted one more chance to melt into his sinewy arms and have a last go 'round just to get him out of her system.

"You thinkin' what I'm thinkin'?" she whispered in his ear. He began to dance her toward the back door. "I'm way ahead of you, Darlin'." He whispered back, and his hot breath on her ear made her dizzy…or it could have been the enormous amount of beer she'd drunk…hard to tell.

The couple virtually raced to his pickup. Before they got in, he pushed her up against the cab as they kissed and groped, and giggled between heavy panting breaths. He finally got his keys dug out of his tight jeans and he flung open the pickup door. They climbed in like children up a ladder on a slide.

"Let's get to my place. And hurry!" She snuggled up to him and bit his earlobe.

"That's *way* too far away. Right here and now. I can't wait." He pushed her down onto the big seat and began working at the snap of her jeans. Every impulse she had wanted to go for it, but even after drinking all night, she still didn't want to do the deed in the parking lot of the place she worked. She could hear voices a few cars over. People were coming and going from the bar and anyone could come right up to Coop's pickup windows and watch the show. She was a lot of things, but she wasn't one for public demonstrations. Worse yet, what if Big Dan saw them. No. No way! Not in the parking lot.

"I can't. We can't do it here. We have to go to my place. Or yours. Just not here.

"Come on, Babe, no one cares. No one's looking. Don't worry. It won't take me that long." He kissed a line down her neck and darn it was hard to stick to her guns, but she had already come to a decision.

"No. I can't. Not here." She pushed him away…gently, but still, it was a push. She meant it. She just couldn't do it here.

He stopped, then grinned and the look on his face turned to a smirk. "Why, you afraid you gonna ruin your reputation?" Then he laughed, but it wasn't a friendly laugh. It was mean.

"What in the heck is that supposed to mean?" She scooted back and sat up. He grabbed her by her hips and pulled her back down.

"Don't worry your pretty little red head about it. Now let's get those pants off."

She pushed again, harder this time. And she swatted his hands away, too. "No. You tell me what you meant by that." She sat up, crossed her arms over her chest and waited, glaring at him.

"I meant you're just a waitress at a bar. It's not like you're anyone special. You probably have a go with half the customers that come into the place." His eyes narrowed and smirked. Obviously, if he couldn't have his way, he was going to grind her self esteem into the dirt beneath his boot. It was exactly the kind of thing her Daddy would have done.

It felt like all the air in the pickup cab disappeared. She couldn't get out of the truck fast enough. He hopped out of the truck, too, and met her as she came around to head back into the bar.

"Oh, come on. I was just teasin'. You're not gonna get mad at me? You're not gonna leave." He reached out, grabbed her arm, and spun her around.

"Don't touch me!" She yelled, her feet planted and her hands in fists, ready to fight. She glanced around for other people, but now the parking lot was empty.

"You're my gal and I'll touch you if I please." He pulled her toward him and grabbed her other arm. "You can't tease a man like that and then say no." His voice dripped with threats and his eyes burned. He held her there with his fingers digging into her arms.

"Let me go, Coop."

He didn't.

"I mean it!" She raised her voice and tried to pull away, but he held on tighter.

"No, we're going to talk about this then finish what we started. " He turned and pulled her behind him as he went to open the pick up door. "We're gonna sit here in this truck and straighten this out, then you *will* give me what I need."

"No. I will not!" Chicky yelled as she pulled as hard as she could and jerked out of his hands. She almost fell down on the gravel in the parking lot, but she caught herself and spun around. "This is it. No more. We're done." She was breathing heavy, fear and anger twisting a knot in her gut.

"What's this? You're dumping me?" Wild disbelief flared in his eyes.

She turned, determined to stomp back to the bar. She'd said everything she intended to say. Her hands were shaking and her legs felt weak. She had to get away from him. She could tell his temper was about to blow. And then she felt his hand clutch her by the hair.

He started to drag her through the gravel to his pickup as she tried to gain her footing. "No. I'll tell *you* when this relationship is done, bitch. And *you* do not walk away from *me*." Chicky had managed to turn herself around and she dug her fingernails into his hand. He let go with a yelp but reached out one last time to grab and pull her upright by her arm. She saw his other arm pull back and then his hand came at her face. She jerked her head away, but his knuckles still landed hard on her eye. He came back with a second slap, with the palm of his hand now, and she crumpled to the ground, her head swimming, and her eye throbbing.

He stood above her, one foot on her either side, ready to hit her again if he needed to. She covered her face, afraid to say anything, but knowing she had to be still to avoid more of his rage. He stood there for a moment, towering above her like a lion above his kill, his hands clenching and unclenching as his chest heaved in a mixture of anger and some kind of sick delight. And then, as fast as it started, it was done. He turned, walked away, got into his pickup, and spun out, spitting gravel from his tires back at her.

She lay quietly until she heard the roar of his truck speed off into the distance. Silence settled around her. She sat up and reached to touch her swelling eye. It hurt like hell. Now what?

Dust Yourself Off and Take a Deep Breath

Maybe this was over. Maybe he got the hint she wouldn't be as easy to control as other women he'd bruised before. Maybe tonight he'd burn off his anger…drink more or sober up…but what she really wanted right then was for him to drive his truck off a cliff and burst into flames when it crashed at the bottom of a ravine. Then she hoped he was still alive and coyotes would come along and gnaw at him. Then she hoped he was *still* alive, but just enough to feel the rats eating off his face!

Snap out of it, Chicky. She crossed herself and apologized to God for thinking such horrible things, but she couldn't help it. The memories of her mother burned a hole in her heart where forgiveness used to live. She said she'd never let a man hit her and here she was, lying in the dirt and gravel of the parking lot of The GiddyUp. She stood up, dusted off her jeans, and took a deep breath. The hope of him moving on made her feel better. The thought of him beating up other women got her Levi's in a twist.

Her inner-bitch rose to the surface as she stomped toward the bar to go in and splash water on her swelling face. The more she thought about Coop getting away with beating up on women, the more infuriated she became. "No damn man is gonna get away with hitting me." She mumbled as gravel crunched beneath her furious stomps. She was still weaving from the night of drinking, but there was nothing like getting smacked around to sober up a girl darn quick.

92

Then she ran right into Big Dan. He was coming out to check the parking lot for fights, just a few minutes too late. She looked up and even in the dim light of the blinking neon sign, she could tell by the surprise on his face he noticed her swelling eye.

He grabbed her arm. "Slow down. What happened?" His worry-barometer shot to the top and she could tell he was putting two and two together. "Did that ass hit you?"

She tugged her arm away and marched into the bar. Dan was right on her heels. "Chicky. Tell me what happened!" She could hear the panic in his voice. He wasn't going to let this go.

She spun to face him. "Mind your own business, Dan! I mean it. I've taken all the crap from men I intend to this evening!" She covered her fear with anger, an emotion far easier to deal with.

She tried to get to the bathroom, but he moved in front of her. "Chicky. You're not going anywhere until you tell me what happened to your eye." He leaned in to look her over for more bruises.

"No." She said as calmly as she could muster and she turned her face away from him. "I'm not talking about it at all. Not tonight. And not here." Then she pleaded with him with her one good eye. "Please, Dan?" she asked. "I really just want to go home." She could feel defeat coming. Chicky Torres could handle hard work. She could handle an argument with anyone. She could take care of herself. But she couldn't stand to cry in front of people. She'd rather scream and shout and shake her fists than let anyone see her weak side. But the tears were beginning to brim and she felt a quiver taking over her chin. Going to the bathroom was no longer her destination. She needed to go home, pronto. "I don't want to cry in public." The knot in her throat was starting to choke her. The dam was about to burst. "Let me go, Dan."

Dan looked like he was about to erupt into tears himself. She had always suspected he was a big marshmallow, and now she had her proof. He reluctantly stepped aside and she began to leave. Behind her she heard him say, "I'm here for you. Don't forget. I'm always here for you." She shook her head and held up her hand in acknowledgment as she went through the big double doors, leaving the safety of people and the undying affection of Big Dan Tanner behind. She put her little truck in drive and pointed her headlights toward home. One last glance in her rearview mirror showed Dan, watching her leave, but looking like he wanted to run after her.

When she got home, she took a good long soak in the tub. Two ibuprofen and an ice pack for her eye and she was off to bed. Unfortunately, sleep didn't come. Finally, she gave up and called Dan.

"You didn't do anything stupid like go hunt down Coop, did you?" She asked when he picked up. He was silent. "Dan! Talk to me."

"No, I didn't do anything. I can't just run around beating people up when I don't even know the whole story. *You* talk to *me*!" He sounded ticked. She started to cry. Alone in her room, she could cry all she wanted.

"Oh, no. Don't do that." She could hear the agony in Dan's voice. No self-respecting man liked to hear a gal cry. She tried to shut off the water works, but the tears wouldn't stop. She pulled the big yellow Chenille bedspread up to her neck.

"Should I come over?" Dan asked. Hopeful.

Maybe she should let him. Maybe he was just what she needed. "No. I just wanted to talk to someone. I'm sorry. I'll try to stop blubbering like a baby."

He was quiet. "It's ok. I'll listen." Devotion swelled in his words. Such a good man, she thought.

"It was Coop. He hit me." She paused after her confession. Hearing the words out loud felt like a secret she wasn't supposed to tell. Like the secret her mother kept from her own extended family all those years ago. Like the secret Chicky kept to herself when she was little, because if the other kids knew about how her Daddy hit her Mamma, maybe they wouldn't like her.

"I figured as much." Dan said. "You want me to find him and teach him what it feels like to get a real beating? I'd be more than happy to do it."

"No, Dan. Don't. I don't want you cleaning up my messes. I want to have a hand in his punishment. I'm not sure what I'm going to do yet, but I know one thing. I plan to teach that bastard a lesson to last him the rest of his lifetime. I will take some help with my plan though, if you're willing."

"I'm your man." Dan's enthusiasm resounded with determination. She knew he meant more than just for this task.

When she told him, "I know," she decided it was time she took him seriously.

The Morning After

Leaning against her sink, Chicky stared at her swollen purple and brown eye. Her fingers curled around the edge of the vanity as she studied her reflection and felt the fire of her anger creep up her neck. She'd always said she would never be at the back of anyone's hand, but here she was. And she hadn't even gone Taz on him. That disappointed her as much as anything. She lay there and took it. Not as much as a kick to his groin. She didn't expect it all to happen so quickly…or to be so terrifying.

So what was she going to do about it? The more she thought about it, the more inflamed she became. No use staring at her bruised mug. Now was not the time to feel bad for herself. That wasn't her style anyway. Now was the time to teach that ass a lesson he'd remember every day of his life. She was the kind of girl who wouldn't stop thinking until she had a plan, and although she wasn't sure how she'd make him pay, she did know she would have to get him alone to do it. A little dinner for two started forming in her mind.

The phone rang. She ran over to check and saw Coop's cell number filling in the caller ID window. No time like the present. "Hello," she said, her voice small and shaking, trying to sound frail and frightened.

"Oh, Chicky. Darlin', I'm so sorry." She heard his weak attempt to sound like he was sobbing. "I have no idea what came over me. You have to believe me; I'm not normally like that." He paused. "I just had a really bad day at work, and girl, you got me so riled up in that truck and when you pulled away…well, I just lost myself for a moment. You understand don't you? Please tell me you understand." He was talking fast, trying to dig himself out of a hole like a whining brat. Too late – she was pissed and now there would be hell to pay.

"I do, Coop. I do believe you," She almost puked at the taste of her lie. "It was my fault, really. I can't blame you at all." She wasn't too bad an actress if she did say so herself. She could hear the pathetic tone in her voice and wondered if he'd fall for it. "You had every right to be mad at me. I need to apologize to you, if anyone needs to apologize at all." She stopped for a while to see if he took the bait.

"Well now, sugar. Don't worry about it. What's done is done. Let's just move on." She could hear smug justification in his voice. *Prick.* "Why don't we talk about how you're gonna make it up to me." He slipped into that low suggestive tone that once wrapped her around his finger, but now made her skin crawl.

"Oh, I'm in the process of planning something very special for you. Just get that tight little butt of yours over here tonight 'round seven. I'm making a fresh pot of Killer Chili with your name all over it."

Hey Good Lookin', Whatcha Got Cookin'?

Home from the grocery store, she tied the red and white checked apron around her narrow waist, Chicky checked the clock. One o'clock. She had plenty of time to make an unforgettable meal. She planned to come up with an idea to make him think twice about hitting a girl again. She also wanted to make sure he knew, from the first bite to the last, what he would be missing out on when he lost her.

First things first. She got out all of her ingredients, the kettle she inherited from her *abuela*, and a bottle of beer. Her little farmhouse didn't have air conditioning, and on this hot day, between the spices in the chili, the temperature of the stove, and the fire burning in her heart, things were going to heat up.

She poured oil in the old kettle and, as it heated, she thought about the sting of the blows Coop dealt her. She'd never been hit before and now she had a whole new appreciation for all the beatings her mother took. The pot sizzled and popped when she dropped diced onion into the oil. She stirred the Spanish yellow until it became translucent in the bubbling fat. Five minced cloves of garlic dribbled in from her fingers – sure to kill him if being a vampire was what drove him to be a creep. Then she shook a healthy teaspoon full of red pepper flakes into the pot, and the spiced steam filled the kitchen with a peppered aroma.

Chicky wiped her forehead with the back of her arm as she diced bacon into small bits. Her eye was still swollen. *Good.* She wanted Coop to see the damage he had done. She tossed the bacon into the sizzling pot and even though she was mad as a wet hen, she could still appreciate the smell of bacon and garlic. Cooking was balm for her soul.

While the bacon browned, Chicky took a long pull from the cold beer. It had to be close to ninety-five degrees outside. Luckily, her yard was shaded. Boone looked up at her with hungry eyes.

"Oh Boone, I haven't forgotten about you."

She grabbed leftover grilled rib steak from the fridge and carved away the fat. She tossed Boone a small piece and he caught it mid air. "Good dog." He licked his chops and waited, hoping for more, but she diced up the rest of it and tossed it into the pot.

While the bacon continued to brown, she wandered out on her front porch with Boone and her beer. She looked out at the garden shed and thought about the tools it held. Hammers, shears, a hoe, a shovel, a rake. She really wanted to make that ass pay for hitting her, but she knew she didn't have the strength to beat him up with a yard tool. She shook her head and laughed at herself as she toyed with the mental image of her chasing Coop around with a shovel. The smell of bacon reached her nose. Time to add the ground beef and pork sausage.

Moving back into the kitchen, she broke up the meat into the cooking pot as she continued to mull over what was in the garden shed. Fertilizer, weed killer, plant food…all would probably make that boy pretty darn sick if not dead. She smiled. Dead was probably going overboard, but darn it, she knew no matter what she did to teach him a lesson, he was bound to go back out and bully some other poor gal. It seemed to her, she thought, as she sprinkled flour over the now-browned meat mixture, she was going to need to figure out how to leave a lasting impression on Coop if she really wanted to change his ways.

Chicky opened the cans of beef consommé and diced tomatoes. She dumped them into the floured meat and stirred until it formed a nice thick sauce. Chicky grabbed her jar of smoked paprika and as she stirred in a heavy-handed pour, the color turned a rich burnt-red. She was still stumped, but knew she couldn't let Coop get away with what he'd done to her, and what he'd surely do to others.

She wandered back outside while the pot stewed. Chicky was almost done with her beer and she wondered what kind of things might be in her garage. Oil, gasoline, a stack of newspapers she needed to take to the recycling center…*hmm*… *maybe a fire*? She imagined him tied to a stake with a bonfire below him. The image put a big smile on her face, but she doubted she was capable of such torture.

It seemed, as she cooked and drank beer, her fury began to fizzle, and she wondered if she would be able to go through with her plan after all. She grabbed the smoked sea salt and added it and then cumin to the pot, and she threw in some white and black pepper while she was at it. As she stirred, she realized she was humming "Stand By Your Man." *Shoot*. She surely wasn't going to go soft on this guy, was she?

But what if hitting her *was* an isolated incident?

Maybe she was just the woman he needed to help him figure out how to deal with his anger. She dumped a can of refried beans into the pot, a dash or two of Worcestershire, and a nice shot of blackstrap molasses, then stirred the thick concoction. Sweat dripped down the side of her face. It must have been at least ninety degrees in the kitchen. Her tank top was soaked through with sweat and stuck to her skin. It was time for another beer and time to let the chili simmer. The top of the beer popped off with a twist and she went out to think and drink, and try to put things into perspective.

On the one hand, he really couldn't be allowed to get away with being a bully. If she didn't let him know his actions were absolutely not acceptable and completely horrible, then someone else who had less strength than she did would end up suffering. On the other hand, she knew she could be a handful, too. Maybe it was a little her fault. Maybe she did push him too far. They'd been drinking and he probably *did* think she was being unreasonable. She finished off her second beer and felt a little light-headed, but in a good way, what with the weight of the troubles on her mind. Then she remembered she had more cooking to do.

Time to add the chili powder. At the very back of her spice cupboard sat a big old Mason jar. Chicky kept it full of her special blend of chili spices. She made it once every two months and twice a month during chili competition season. No one knew the ingredients to her kick-ass chili powder and no one ever would. She guarded that concoction like it was filled with gold. She carefully brought the jar down and unscrewed the old metal lid. One heaping tablespoon was all she needed. The even, penetrating heat it brought made the true chili connoisseur sweat just the right amount, remember it for a couple hours after tasting it, but not suffer third degree burns. It was a fine spice blend and she was proud of it. She gave the pot a good stir, turned the heat to low, and left it so the tastes could meld together. This chili won her the three golden peppers sitting on the dresser in her bedroom. She would never tamper with this chili recipe. No ingredient changes ever for Chicky's Killer Chili. It was perfect. Now, it was time to get ready for her dinner guest, and time to finally figure out a plan so Cooper Wolfe could get a taste of his own medicine.

Dinner For Two

By the time Coop rang the doorbell, the house had cooled off and Chicky had managed to look like a million bucks with a big, black eye. She didn't put on a stitch of makeup to cover the purple brown stain. Clean and natural, the way she usually presented herself anyway. She let her shoulder-length red hair dry naturally, resulting in ringlets of curls framing her face. Just the way her *abuela* always said she looked best.

When she answered the door, she could tell she got the outfit right by the initial look on Coop's face. A white tank top, low cut, her cut off denim shorts fringe tickling the top of her long thighs. Barefoot with light pink toenails, Chicky knew she looked good enough to take a bite out of and that was her goal. She wanted to show this idiot what he would be missing.

She had decided she had to go through with her plan. She had found the perfect tool out in the shed. When she went out to look, there it was, spectacular and ideal – an old branding iron with a big double B on it for Bullying Bastard. (Double B ranch actually, but he didn't need to know that.) She had it sitting on a hot plate in her bathroom. The door was shut and a candle burned in the bedroom to mask any smells of heating metal. She planned to brand his woman-beating ass so he'd never forget what she thought of him. She figured he'd try to beat the living hell out of her, but that is where Big Dan came in. He'd be there to save her. She had told Dan to be outside her house at nine o'clock. She planned to label Coop for life around ten minutes after nine, and although she was prepared to run like a jackrabbit once the metal touched his bum, she didn't want to take any chances.

Coop, as always, looked at her chest first, then down the length of her, and he licked his lips. It wasn't until he glanced up to make eye contact that he saw her shiner.

She expected him to wince, draw back, apologize…at least look like he had one frigging ounce of regret. But, no. What she saw affirmed the branding iron heating in the bathroom. The bastard smiled. Just a little. A wee bit of pride or power showed in his eyes and on his mouth, right before he cleared his throat, reached up and pasted a serious look onto his face. He reached out and touched her bruise with the thumb of his hand then slid his fingers into her hair. He pulled her to him and kissed her as though the sight of her bruise turned him on. It was all she could do not to knee him in his tender spot, but his kiss was of that passionate variety which had drawn her to him in the first place. Knowing what she had in mind for him gave her the courage to kiss him back like she meant it.

"I'm glad you're here," she said as she placed her hands on his chest and pushed away playfully. "I've made you a fresh pot of chili, a pan of cornbread and strawberry shortcake for dessert."

"Oh, all my favorites," he winked and took a few more kisses as he backed her into the house, holding her tight. Her brains were having a hell of a time controlling her emotions. This guy could wrap her around his finger so easily. Too easily.

"This is dessert enough for me, though," he nibbled her ear and she melted a little. Oh hell. She melted a lot.

No. He hit me. This bastard hit me. I need to get my head on straight. Why is he being so damn sexy?

She pulled away completely. "Help yourself to a beer. I'll be right back." She sashayed away to the bathroom to check on the branding iron. It was nice and hot, and smoking a little. She opened the window then stared at herself in the mirror.

Chicky Torres, what have you gotten yourself into? She touched the bruise on her eye and winced. Still tender. She looked in the mirror and at the branding iron behind her. *Really? I'm going to brand his ass?* She really didn't know if she could go through with it. She knew she'd have to get him naked and in the bedroom first. That wouldn't be hard to do. What was bothering her most was she was looking forward to the foreplay before the punishment. *What is wrong with me?* She should hate him. She should want to kill him for hitting her. Is this why women take it? Is this why Mamma stayed in a marriage with split lips and finger-shaped bruises on her upper arms? She had to keep telling herself he would hit her again.

106

Men who hit once will always be capable of hitting again.

"Chicky, I'm getting lonely out here." She heard him calling. She had to stick with her original plan. She put a little cold water on her face and headed back out to try to fool him…and herself.

Unfortunately, they had nothing but wonderful conversation throughout the meal. Coop was especially tender and gentle, although he never said a word about her eye. Neither did she. After all, she'd told him on the phone it was as much her fault as his and they should move on. She glanced at the clock. It was only eight o'clock. Shoot. She had a whole hour to kill. He'd already gobbled up her chili and the cornbread, too. She hoped dessert would last at least forty-five minutes.

Dessert was going to be wonderful. Homemade shortcakes and strawberries picked from her garden. She even used a secret she saw on a TV cooking show and made a simple-syrup with fresh mint leaves from her yard to flavor the whipped cream to top it all off.

When she stood to get dessert, Coop grabbed her hand and pulled her into his lap. "Hold on, girl. I told you what I wanted for dessert." He didn't waste a lot of time. Before she could argue, he was carrying her to the couch.

"Coop…let's go to the bedroom." She had to get him in the bedroom. No way could she get him on his stomach then run across the house to her bathroom and back with a hot branding iron. He wouldn't wait that long. The branding iron would go cold. He'd see her. It simply wouldn't work.

He ignored her and smothered her with lust-filled kisses as he began to peel off his shirt. "Coop…" she managed to beg weakly, but she didn't mean it. She didn't care. Damn. He was like a drug. How could he get to her like this? She wanted this as much as he did. One last time…to gain his trust, she convinced herself.

Soon they were in the throes of some of the best sex she'd had in her life. The energy, the passion…it was completely intoxicating. When done, they were both panting as they lay on the rug in the middle of the living room floor.

"Now that's what I call dessert." He laughed.

She couldn't argue. Regardless of her plans, she now couldn't imagine carrying out what she had originally planned. She'd have chickened out before she did it, she thought, in that dreamy after-sex neutral mode of thinking. Then her mind shifted back into drive.

Crap! Dan!

She looked at the clock – nine p.m. *Oh, no.* By now Dan was waiting outside her bedroom window ready to charge in and rescue her. She moved to stand up. She had to tell Dan to leave. She had to tell him she couldn't go through with it.

She had forgiven Coop. At that moment, she honestly believed he would never hit her again. How could he? They had too much of a connection. She could figure out how to tame him.

But, before she could get up, Coop grabbed her arm and pulled her back down. "I need seconds." His grin was devilish but his grip was rough.

"No, I can't. I have to go to the bathroom." Chicky tried to pull away only to have him pull her back, but forcefully this time, his fingers squeezing tight on her upper arm.

"Oh, no you don't. I'm having seconds and you're not going to say no to me. Remember what happened last time you said, no." He rolled her over and hovered above her, his smile now a smirk and his eyes dark and smoldering, with something in those eyes so familiar. They were the eyes she had seen just the night before.

"Coop, no, I really need to go. She tried to push him, but he held steady.

"You're not going to tease me and stop like you did the other night…are you? I thought you learned your lesson. 'Cause I don't like being teased. You *know* that. You know what the punishment is for that, right?" His voice went cold and the smile left him.

Her heart clenched in her chest. *This* was the man who had backhanded her. *There* was the temper she remembered, building on his face. Her mouth dropped open. He was serious. The bastard was serious. One moment she was stupid enough to forgive him and now all she wanted was to get her hands on that branding iron. The way he gripped her arms, she wondered if she could get away. *Think, Chicky, think.*

She softened her voice and eyes. "Now, Coop. I have every intention of having seconds and thirds and even fourths if you want, but I honestly have to pee right now!" She stroked his face. "Plus, I want to be in bed where it's soft. This floor is too hard." She twirled his hair in her fingers and saw his face relax. He sighed and let go of her arms then sat up.

"Ok. I suppose if nature calls, I can wait."

Chicky hopped up while she had the chance. "You're a doll." And off she ran to get her cast iron label-maker and get back to her original plan.

When she got to the bedroom, she locked the door and leaned back against the cool wood while she panted, her mind racing. He wasn't going to like it when he found the door locked, and it would likely piss him off, but she had to talk to Dan. She threw on a robe, cinched it up tight, and went to her bedroom window and pulled back the curtain. There was Dan, waiting, smacking a baseball bat against his enormous hand.

"Dan. Thank goodness you're here!" She whispered out the window.

Dan startled. "'Course I'm here. Is it time?" He turned and squinted into the window looking at her. She pulled the robe tight around her neck and tried to smooth the matted hair at the back of her head.

"No…not yet. Uh…there was a glitch."

"I can see." His crossed his arms over his chest and cleared his throat.

Chicky blushed and felt terrible, but she didn't have time for that now. "I have to get him into bed."

"Yeah, yeah. I know!" He whisper-yelled. "I'm right here outside the window. I'll hear. Just get to it. I'm ready." He turned his back to the window, clearly jealous.

Chicky ran to the bathroom. The iron was hotter than hell and ready to leave its mark. All she had to do was convince him to let her give him a peppermint oil back massage. She had made it herself…again with her fresh mint. She sprayed the sheets with peppermint fragrance, dropped the robe to the floor, and went to let him in.

There he was, in the kitchen, gobbling up the strawberry shortcake, piled high with what looked to be all of the mint whipped cream she'd made.

"Damn, this is good Chicky. I ate the entire bowl of whipped cream. It is so different, I can't figure out why, but it's soooo good." He sauntered over, seductively sucking a dollop of whipped cream from his finger. "Too bad I didn't save some for us to play with."

"Well come on in, my man. I have a plan for you way hotter than anything you could have done with that whipped topping."

He grinned from ear to ear and followed, puppy-like, a little whipped cream on his upper lip.

Behind her, she heard him cough. She looked back at him and his face looked a little red. He sure was getting all worked up. She was going to have to make this good.

"Now you lay down on your stomach. I'm going to give you a hot oil massage you will never, ever forget."

He smiled a little, but coughed again, winced as he held his stomach and became redder yet. He seemed almost dizzy. A little sick, maybe?

She couldn't care less. *Just lay down you woman-beating barbarian.*

"Ok," he said, but his eyes had an odd look to them. Did he suspect something? He went to the bed and laid down on his stomach, his fine, tight fanny glowing in the candlelight.

"I'm going to go get the oil." Chicky left and he didn't say a word. Apparently, he was already completely relaxed, his stomach full and who knows, maybe she'd get lucky and he'd fall asleep. That would make this whole thing a lot easier.

When she got to the bathroom, she paced. Could she do this? Could she really cause pain and harm to a man? She stared in the mirror. He sure as hell hadn't worried about the pain he caused her. She stared at the branding iron. She paced some more. She couldn't keep stalling. She paced a little more, then slipped into her clothes and tied up her sneakers as she wouldn't be able to make a run for it stark naked and barefoot, and she knew she'd have to run fast. She picked up the handle of the branding iron. The iron was red hot. She looked over into the mirror at her eye. She thought about her mother and all the beatings she took. She thought about how he looked as though he was about to hit her only minutes ago. Yes. Not only could she do it, she couldn't wait.

"I hope you're ready for something really hot," she said with a sing-song lilt as she opened the door to the bathroom and snuck out with the branding iron, holding it like a spear she was about to throw. She literally had to strike while the iron was hot, as they say.

She went to the bed…he lay perfectly still. Sleeping as she'd hoped. She readied the iron. He didn't say a word. What luck. Well, this would wake him but good! She focused. She had to do this. With one determined motion, she brought the red-hot iron down to the flesh of his tight, round buttock and pressed with determination. She would leave a mark for all to see! She smelled his flesh singe on impact, but he didn't as much as move a muscle.

"What the hell?" Chicky gasped, as she pulled the iron away. The large BB brand stared up at her, smoldering, smelling like some kind of twisted bacon, but Coop lay perfectly still.

"Coop?" She quaked, confusion and fear creeping into her brain. No one would have lain still for that. No one!

She walked up to his shoulder and looked at his face. His eyes stared straight at her, and his mouth lolled open, a little foam at his lips, his stare completely vacant.

She reached forward with one hand, the branding iron still tightly gripped in her other, and shook his shoulder. "Coop?" She waited. Nothing.

Dear God. He was dead.

At first she stared, slack-jawed and wide-eyed, and then she felt the scream building in her chest and finally escaping from her lips.

"Dan!"

Big Dan Bursts In

Dan burst into Chicky's bedroom, waving the baseball bat tightly gripped in his white-knuckled fist, ready to crack heads. Chicky was still screaming, but in between her yelps of horror she began to blabber a mile a minute. She waved and pointed and pulled at her hair. "Dan. He's dead. Oh, holy hell, I swear I didn't mean to kill him. I don't know why he's dead, but he is. I didn't know it. I swear if I'd have known he was dead, I wouldn't have put the iron to him!"

Dan's eyes locked on the red welt on Coops round butt cheek and winced.

"He didn't feel it. He never even flinched. Dan, I swear, he was dead before I branded him." She shook her head and clasped her hands together, pleading for him to believe her.

Dan stared at her, then the man's ass, then back to her and then a strange look came over his face and he started to laugh. At first he covered his mouth and tried hard to stifle it, but soon he was shaking, and not long after he was bent over, hands on his knees, gasping for breath as tears rolled down his ruddy cheeks.

"Dan! What has gotten into you! This is serious. Very serious!" She'd never seen Dan laugh so hard. The man was hysterical. Then she looked at Coop's ass, then to Dan, then back to Coop's ass and she felt the giggles coming on. "Oh, shit." She giggled more, and soon she had her own confused tears of laughter running down her heated cheeks. The two of them melted to the floor of her bedroom, a baseball bat, and a branding iron between them, as they tried to quell their morbid fits of hilarity.

"Chicky," Dan finally had a grip on himself. "This is serious. What in the hell happened?" He was still wiping his eyes. "Did you add any extra, *special* spices to your chili tonight?"

Chicky gasped. "I most certainly did not! Dan! I absolutely did not mean to kill the man. I just wanted him to learn a lesson." Chicky shook her head, appalled Dan would think her capable of murder.

"Sorry, sorry." He held his hands palm up in apology. "I'm just trying to figure out what killed him, Chicky. He was awful young for a heart attack, and you said he was dead before you branded him. He just about had to choke or die of some other cause."

Chicky lowered her voice like she didn't want the dead guy to hear. "I know. I mean, I sure as hell wouldn't have branded him if I'd have thought for a minute he was dead...or dying...or whatever." Chicky stood up. She stared at the back end of the cowboy and sighed. "Now look at this! How in the hell am I gonna explain this to authorities?" She spun back to face Dan with fear in her eyes. "Dan! I'm going go to jail for murder and I didn't even murder him. How in the hell am I ever going to explain this! Who would believe any of it?"

Dan stood and went to put his arm around Chicky, but didn't say anything. He was deep in thought. He went over to look into Coop's dead face. He checked his eyes and craned his neck to peek over his shoulder. Chicky could tell he didn't want to touch him.

"I just can't for the life of me figure out why this guy would have died all of sudden like this. I mean," he turned to look into Chicky's eyes, "are you *sure* it wasn't something he ate?"

Chicky searched her mind for the answer and half mumbled, "Well, unless he was allergic to something. I ate everything he ate." She began to tick off the meal on her fingers. "We had some chips and salsa before dinner…but that was out of a jar and a bag. I ate them. I'm fine. We had chili and cornbread and I ate both of those things, too. Tea. He had a beer. Dan…I can't imagine…" then her eyes lit up and her hand snapped up and over her mouth when she remembered. "Wait! He had strawberry shortcake, too. I *didn't* have that." Then she shook her head. "No, now wait. I ate some of the strawberries when I was making it. The shortcake was homemade and I nibbled some of it earlier in the day." Chicky shook her head then added, "Course, there was the whipped cream." She looked up with wide eyes. "It had to be the whipped cream, Dan!"

"How did you make it?"

"Whipping cream with mint-flavored simple syrup. It smelled wonderful," and then her mouth dropped open," but I never tasted it! Dan. He got here right as I was finishing it up and I never tasted it." This didn't make any sense to her. "Why would mint-flavored whipped cream kill him?"

"Mint?" Dan's mouth dropped open. "Please tell me you didn't pick the mint out of your yard."

Chicky's eyes widened and she put her fists on her hips. "Of course I picked the mint from my yard. Why would I go buy mint when I have a whole patch of it? Do you think he was allergic to it? Is that it? Dan! Talk to me! What the hell are you thinking?"

Dan scrubbed his face with his now shaking hands and inhaled deeply, then moaned as he trudged out of the bedroom. She followed on his heels. "Dan. You're scaring me. What's going on?"

The only thing that came to her mind as she puzzled over the mint was how many cutworms had been all over it this season. Darned bugs, she worried they were going to kill the plant and she'd just been talking to Dan about how she needed to get her hands on some serious insecticide to kill those…

"Oh, no!" Chicky groaned and slapped her hand over her mouth. "Dan. Did you do me a favor this week that you forgot to tell me about?"

Dan swallowed hard as he leaned heavily on the counter in her kitchen. He nodded his head, but couldn't look up to make eye contact.

"I sprayed the hell out of that mint with some old Furadan I found in the back of my garage. I was gonna tell you, but I forgot. Then this whole thing with Coop came up and it slipped my mind." He looked up and when his eyes met hers, she began to back away, shaking her head in disbelief. "Chicky! How could I know you'd put mint in the whipped cream? Who does that?"

Dan began pacing, his fingers digging into his thick hair. Chicky looked away from him and back into her room, the candle light still flickering its reflection off Coop's branded ass. She had a dead guy in her bed and a big guy falling apart at her counter. She decided she couldn't take the heat. It was time to get out of the kitchen.

Now What?

Chicky wandered to her front porch and sat on the steps, staring up at the night sky. It was around ten o'clock and they had a full, dark night ahead of them to figure out what to do. Her brain churned with ideas that surprised even her. Mostly she was just trying to figure out how she was going to tell her mamma she was going to jail.

The screen door banged and she scooted over to make room for Dan. He sat down with a heavy sigh, then leaned forward with his head cradled in his hands. They sat in silence for a long time, both of them staring into the black night, deep in thought and worry.

"I can't report this to the authorities, Dan. I just can't see a way I won't be suspected of murder. It was my mint that killed him and obviously, I had intent to harm the man…that brand isn't going to disappear." Chicky leaned back and stared at Dan, waiting for his response.

Dan nodded. "I know. I agree. Technically, I'm an accomplice, so I'm not thrilled with the idea either." Then silence.

A few minutes passed. "So what do I do, Dan? What do I do?" Her voice quivered. She felt tears brimming in her eyes and she squeezed them shut and pinched her arm to try to stifle the onslaught of water. Now was no time to be a weak girl about things.

Dan looked in her watery eyes, leaned over, and kissed her forehead. "I'll take care of things. It's me who murdered the man with Furadan. I should have told you I sprayed the mint. Actually, I should have beaten the tar out of Coop when I saw that bruised eye of yours last night." He paused and she could hear him take a deep breath and swallow hard. "But more than that, I should have made you stop looking for other men a long time ago. You know damn well no one will ever love you as much as I do."

There would be no more stopping her tears. She let the damn burst and she sobbed like a three year-old. Dan wrapped her up in his arms as they sat in the dark on her front porch.

Chicky looked up into his eyes. Kind eyes. Loving eyes. How had she not seen this before? Why had she been so sure he wasn't the right man for her? It shouldn't have taken something like this for her to wake up and recognize a good man when she saw one. She stretched up to kiss him. A real kiss. Their first kiss. Warm lips. His beating heart beneath her hand. And sparks. She hadn't expected sparks. He sat very still as she kissed him. The hand she had gently laid against his cheek felt his tears. She pulled away to look at him. His smile, grateful and genuine, said all the words he'd been trying to tell her through his actions since she moved here. She was blind, but now she could see. Too bad it had taken something like this to make her finally come to her senses.

He cleared his throat and wiped his face. "Well, although I'm thrilled you have finally seen the light, I don't think this is the time for smoochin'." Dan laughed. "I never thought I'd say those words to you." He laughed more and Chicky joined him as she blushed. "We've got to deal with old branded-ass in there, and turning ourselves in can't be part of it."

As if the nightmare they were going through wasn't bad enough, they saw headlights about a mile down the gravel road, coming their way.

"Shit!" Dan stood up quick. "No one ever drives down this road." He leapt from the porch and headed to Coop's truck parked right in her driveway. "I'm gonna put this behind the shed. You go throw some covers over that corpse and shut the door to the bedroom."

Chicky didn't miss a beat. The two were in complete sync with each other. She didn't know who was coming but she did know one thing for sure. She was the only house on this road except for Dan's. The only people she saw on this road were the mail carrier, Dan, or someone coming to visit her or Dan. The chances were fifty-fifty the lights closing in on her house were coming to see her. She flew into the house and took care of her business as Dan, sans headlights, pulled the truck behind the shed and ran back to sit on the porch. Chicky came out as casually as she could, two beers in her shaking hands, just as the county sheriff pulled onto the yard. Dan took the beer from her hand, gave a long hard look at the patrol car, and drank half the beer in one gulp. Chicky, oddly composed, gave the car a little wave as she sat down as though it was perfectly normal to have the sheriff visiting.

"Hey, Rube," Chicky called out as Sheriff Rueben Bader got out of his vehicle.

"Hey, Chicky." Rueben flashed a smile and his gold tooth flickered a reflection from the porch light.

"Come on up and have a beer," Dan offered, tipping the cold one in the sheriff's direction.

The sheriff shook his head. "It looks damn good on a hot night like tonight, but I'm on duty." Rueben approached them and stood in front of Chicky, his face taking on a serious tone.

Chicky was afraid to raise the bottle to her lips. She knew her hands were shaking like crazy, so she put them between her knees and kept a tight grip on her hands and the bottle while she waited.

"Chicky, you see Cooper Wolfe lately?" The sheriff pulled a small notepad from his breast pocket and flipped open the cover, then licked the lead of the pencil.

"Yeah, last night." Chicky nodded. *Don't say any more than you have to, girl.* She remembered how to keep a secret…how to tell a lie to cover the truth. She'd done it from the time she was little to avoid questions about her mamma and daddy.

Sheriff Bader stared at her. "Chicky, is that a shiner you got there?" He leaned in a bit to see.

Chicky nodded and looked down in shame. Dear word, it amazed her that here she sat, feeling guilty about admitting she got smacked by a man more than the fact there was a dead man in her bed. The irony of it all. "Yes, Rueben, it is," she said quietly.

"Cooper Wolfe do that to you?" The crickets chirped and Boone stirred behind them, took a stretch, spun a circle, and lay back down.

"Why you askin', Rube?" Dan spoke for her. "It's not a happy subject. It have anything to do with why you're here?" Chicky could see Dan mustering up the courage to do whatever he had to do to protect her. That big, wonderful man. She felt like she was going to burst into tears again, but she held it together.

The sheriff sighed. "Well, we got a report in tonight he's a wanted man. Killed a woman in Louisiana and is suspected of putting a different gal in the hospital over in Dallas." The sheriff shifted from foot to foot. "It looks as though he left his mark on you, too, Chicky. Am I right?"

Chicky stayed silent, but nodded as she hung her head with the same kind of shame she remembered her Mamma having. "It's the last I saw of him," she looked up. "He beat me up in the parking lot of The GiddyUp, then drove away, leaving me lying in the gravel." She stared at the sheriff, waiting to see if he would believe her partial truth.

The sheriff shook his head. "Nothin' worse than a coward who beats up on women." He put his fist on his hips, just inches away from his gun. "Well, just be aware, we're lookin' for him. He's probably long gone from Tom Green County, but if he's around here yet, we'll try to catch him." The sheriff looked at Dan. "Can you stay with Chicky, just in case Cooper comes around again?"

Dan nodded. "I'll keep her safe." He put his arm around Chicky and looked at her, his face showing his statement was more than just words. It was a promise.

"I'm not worried as long as I've got Dan around." Her eyes returned the promise she planned to keep him around for a good long time.

Chicky and Dan waved to the sheriff as he drove out of the yard. They had a feeling even though they had a lot of work to do yet that night, in the end, they'd come out smelling like a Texas rose…with plenty of thorns.

FOURTH COURSE

JUST DESSERTS

CHOCOLATE CHIP KRISPY COOKIES

1 cup margarine
1 cup oil
1 cup brown sugar
1 cup white sugar
1 egg
2 teaspoons vanilla
1 teaspoon salt
1 teaspoon baking soda
1 teaspoon cream of tartar
3½ flour (may need more, should be stiff)
1 cup rolled oats
1 cup Rice Krispies
16 oz. chocolate chips

Blend margarine and oil and then cream in the sugars. Add egg, salt, baking soda, cream of tartar, and mix. Stir in flour. Last, stir in the oatmeal, Rice Krispies, and chocolate chips. Drop by teaspoons onto lightly greased cookie sheets and bake about 12 minutes at 350 or until lightly browned.

TESSA ARLINGTON

The Perfect Apartment

Three solid months. That's how long Tessa Arlington scoured the Lafayette Square area of St. Louis for a decent apartment she could call home. One she could afford. One without mice or cockroaches. And hey, can a girl get a laundry area she's not afraid to spend more than five minutes in? Seriously.

The place Tessa found was right where she wanted to be – in a hip neighborhood with awesome places to eat and shop. She felt cool just saying, "I live in Lafayette Square." Kinda French sounding. Tessa smiled. Yeah. Kinda French. Didn't hurt that the building was well-kept and solid, with a maintenance man who claimed he'd actually show up when she called him to fix the leaking toilet.

She had put the money down yesterday during her lunch hour. No regrets. She didn't even bother to ask a thing about her neighbors.

That was her first mistake.

Tessa parked her car at the curb and hopped out, ready to move in her last load. The Nova was crammed to the top with loads of clothes, knickknacks, and several boxes of books. She had dishes and cookware in one heavy container and bathroom supplies in another. Standing with her hands on her hips staring at the Tetris arrangement of storage containers, Tessa wondered, *how in the heck did I get so much stuff?* The back seat of her car had at least five big boxes and her trunk was filled with most of her clothes and shoes. A guy from work with a truck showed up after work yesterday and helped her move the big stuff. Moving was a lot of work, to be sure. Nothing would make her happier than if this was the last time she had to uproot her stuff. Three moves in the last year were two moves too many. Tessa liked an adventure, but this gypsy lifestyle was killing her.

Tessa trudged up the sidewalk toward her building, one of several in the apartment complex, each having four apartments. Her apartment was number three on the second floor. Breathing heavily under the weight of an enormous box filled with cookbooks, she backed in through the entry door, and ran smack into one of her neighbors. She almost toppled over when she collided into his solid wall of body. *Geez Buddy, watch where you're goin',* was what she would have liked to have said. But hey, being new in the new building and all, she chose to be nice. "Oops! Sorry 'bout that." Then she turned and got an eyeful of the man blocking her way.

He didn't smile through his thick beard and mustache. He only stared at her with an odd inquisitiveness. Without her asking, he reached to take the box from her arms and held it as though it was light as a bag of marshmallows. The guy was immense. Like six foot and holy shit inches huge.

Tessa gulped at his bulging arms. He stared at her without expression, one eye looking at her and the other eye staring just slightly off to the side.

"Thank you," she said, then she swallowed hard as she waited for him to introduce himself.

Nothing. Not a smile, not a nod, not as much as a grunt. *Who acts like that? Is he stealing my stuff or offering to help me?* Tessa couldn't figure the guy out, and there they stood, taking up the majority of the entry way, just staring at each other in silence.

Tessa's brain kicked in and she began to ramble. "Um. Well. I appreciate the help. Come on upstairs then." She started up the stairs and heard his heavy footsteps as he followed. She began to ramble. Nerves. "That box is really heavy. It's surprising how heavy books are. I'm Tessa Arlington. What's your name?" Tessa was still blathering when they walked into her apartment.

Once in the room, the man with her box was still completely silent, and Tessa turned to look at him. She was struck again by his size. He must have had to duck when he went through her doorway. The room looked smaller with him in it. Tessa pointed to the table where she wanted the box and he plodded over and set it down with a thud. He straightened up and stared at her, and for a moment she thought he'd say something. But no, he still just stood there staring at her like he was waiting for more instructions.

"I'm Tessa," she repeated. "And you are…?" She waited as he shifted from foot to foot and stared at the box he'd just put down as though he was trying to think of the answer.

"Buck Fischer." His low, booming voice reverberated off the plain beige walls. Then he looked at her. He stepped forward, his stare so intense, she felt like she had just stepped into an airport x-ray machine. A pit formed in her stomach and she wondered why she had let a stranger in her apartment. Her father's many reminders to be careful hollered in her brain. *Mace in purse. Purse on floor in bedroom. Huge weird stranger in apartment. Dad would be furious if he could see me now. Idiot!*

Be cool, Tessa. Be cool. "I guess I'd better get back to work," Tessa forced an awkward smile and went out into the hall where it felt more public. She waited for him and he did follow her, albeit slowly, as though he didn't understand why he had to leave. "Well, thanks again," she muttered as she shut the door to the apartment. She smiled and backed up a little. He just stared at her. More uncomfortable silence. Man. This guy was off. She turned and started down the stairs, half wondering if she was just being overly cautious or if he was indeed Sasquatch, all shaved down and living in her apartment building. She heard him thumping along behind her and it occurred to her he might come out to her car and keep trying to help her. *Oh, no.* Now what was she going to do. What would she say? How could she be polite, but also let him know she didn't want anything to do with him?

Before she could decide, she heard a door close behind her. Turning, she saw she was now alone in the entryway of her building. He had disappeared behind the closed door of apartment one. *Huh. All that worrying for nothing.* She shrugged. She really had to stop reading horror stories; they made it too easy for her imagination to get the better of her. Tessa was about to decide he was just a quiet guy when the door across the hall opened a crack. Tessa turned to see a little old woman's eyes peering at her through the gap of the door.

"Hi." She smiled at the woman with a wave, then took a tentative step toward the barely opened door. The door closed with a bang. Then *click* after *click* she heard the many locks unlatching and the slide of a chain. The door opened again and there stood a small old woman with stains on her housedress, thick, smudged glasses, wearing only one fuzzy yellow slipper.

The old woman offered a nervous grimace of a smile, revealing poorly-fitting false teeth. "Come in, come in. Hurry." She whispered loudly as she beckoned with a crooked-finger.

Tessa scooted into the apartment and quickly scanned the room. She knew it was rude to stare but she could hardly help it. Her jaw dropped at the surroundings. Tabloid newspapers covered the tables, every chair overflowed with stuffed animals, candy wrappers littered the kitchen counter, and dozens of baskets of crocheting took up valuable floor space.

132

"You met Buck." The woman finished latching all the locks again and shuffled around to face Tessa, her eyes wide in inquisition. "Did he hurt you?" She wrung her gnarled hands together.

"Hurt me? No. Why do you ask that?" Tessa frowned, hardly able to focus on the little lady in front of her what with so much to look at in the carnival of a room.

"I'm Tessa," she offered her hand.

"Betty Sanderson." She grabbed Tessa's hand with her warm little bent fingers and stretched out Tessa's palm, tracing the lines with her fingers.

Dear word. I suppose she's going to try to tell me my fortune. Tessa shook her head and grinned at the odd situation.

"Well, pleased to meet you, Betty. Now tell me. Where is your other slipper?" Tessa couldn't help but ask. The woman had to be almost eighty and she would probably appreciate someone helping her out.

Betty looked down at her feet through her thick glasses, wiggled her red toenails, then looked back up at Tessa with a toothy grin. "I didn't even realize I only had one on." Then she squinted as she looked around the room in an attempt to locate the missing footwear. "Help me look." The little woman waved her hand, indicating Tessa should follow her.

Tessa started to search around the apartment, looking under the couch, then in the other rooms. Betty followed closely and chattered along the way. "You gotta be careful of Buck. Sometimes he seems like a little kid…kinda slow… then other times he's mean." Her voice was scratchy and thin, like she had a lifetime of cheap cigarettes in her past. "At first I thought he was just a little off, but now I know better."

Tessa found the slipper peaking out from under a sweater lying on the ground in Betty's bedroom. "Found it." Tessa handed it to Betty. "Here you go." She took a moment to glance around Betty's bedroom. Tessa wasn't ready to call the Hoarders hotline, but she was close. This woman needed some help.

"Betty, do you have kids? Family?" Tessa smiled when Betty grabbed Tessa's arm to steady herself as she slipped on the bedroom slipper.

"Naw. No kids. Family's gone. Just me." She stood up and grabbed Tessa's hand. "Thanks for finding my slipper. I swear I'd lose my teeth if I didn't put them in my head every morning!" She laughed and Tessa was hooked. This crazy little lady needed someone to watch out for her and Tessa was already thinking about how she was going to offer to help her clean.

First things first. "You want me to clean your glasses for you?" Tessa asked. She had no idea how Betty could even see out of them and the smudges were really bugging her.

Betty looked up. "That would be nice." There was that smile. What a sweet wrinkled little face.

Tessa plucked a tissue from the box on the nightstand. Betty's shaky hands removed her glasses and handed them over.

"Now, what has Buck done to make you suspicious of him?" Tessa breathed on the glasses, smudged with what must have been days', if not weeks', worth of fingerprints. When she finished cleaning them, she placed them on Betty's nose. It was as though they'd known each other for years.

Betty smiled at Tessa's helpful gesture, but when her thoughts returned to Buck, her face wrinkled up like an angry prune. "Oh, there's been things, alright. He knocks on my door in the middle of the night. And then there's the yelling. Oh, the yelling. And I'm here to tell ya. If you don't lock those doors of yours, he'll just wander into your apartment and eat your food! He ate a whole box of my Ding Dongs once. Those are expensive." Betty frowned. "Those are my special treats! I like my sweets, you know." A scowl took over Betty's face.

Tessa smiled, but doubted Betty could see her smile through those thick glasses. "I can't blame you for being upset about that. But how do you know it has been Buck?"

"I just do." Betty gave a confident nod and turned to leave the room.

Tessa followed as she mulled over the things Betty said, and craned her neck to take in the whole freak show that was Betty's apartment. She would need a lot of cleaning supplies when she came to help the little old woman tidy up.

"Now, you come down and see me sometimes. Borrow sugar, visit, that kind of thing. We'll look out for each other." They were at the front door. Betty took both of Tessa's hands in hers and gave them a squeeze. Tessa thought about her own gran. It was going to be nice to have someone to watch out for.

"I will come visit, Betty. Often." Betty smiled a big warm smile and Tessa left her apartment with a good feeling about life, and no more thoughts about the monstrosity of a man who carried her cookbooks into her apartment.

These two odd events weren't going to change the way she felt about her new home. Sure there was a hulking lurch of a character who silently stared a hole through her, and a little old crazy lady with a jillion locks on her door who told her the big guy was bad news...but hey. It was the city. And Tessa was determined to embrace city living.

* * *

By the end of the first week in her apartment, Tessa understood Betty's suspicions about Buck. What Betty had said was true. Each night, from about ten o'clock until around two o'clock in the morning, Buck screamed at the top of his lungs.

Not occasional hollers. Constant, muffled screams and curses that kept Tessa tossing and turning, unable to sleep. No matter how much she paced her floors trying to figure out what to do, she couldn't work out what his problem could possibly be. Nightmares? Or maybe he was on the phone arguing with someone. Could have this been some kind of rage therapy? Nothing really made sense and, honestly, if he hadn't been monster-sized, she would have been downstairs banging on his door by now, telling him to shut the heck up. But adding his size and obvious anger issues to Betty's forewarnings kept Tessa pacing the floor behind her locked door, wondering if this was going to be a constant thing.

It was. And then it got worse.

It was a Tuesday. Buck had wound up to a tirade around 11:30 that night. It was now an hour and a half later. Tessa had tossed and turned until her covers were stripped and her mind was frazzled. Oh, he was in rare form that night. It was the third time in the last hour she found herself flipping on the lights to her living room to wear the tread of that carpet. The first thing she saw when the light flicked on was a manila envelope slid under her front door. She crept toward it…delivered probably within the last fifteen minutes. She opened it, dreading what she would find…her exhausted mind conjuring up nothing but the worst-case scenarios. Black and white photos of her little brother with a blindfold on in a dingy room…Send one million dollars. Or worse. Someone's finger.

Stop reading horror stories.

What *was* inside was a drawing like something
a child would make for his mommy. A large stick
figure holding a big box, and the smaller stick
figure with a big smile on its large round circle of a
head. Tessa groaned. What was this? She dragged
her exhausted body to the couch to stare at the
picture and try to make some sense of it. She felt as
though she should stick the picture on the fridge
with a magnet. One part of her thought it was oddly
cute, but a bigger part of her – the part who heard
Buck screaming downstairs at that very minute –
made her want to tear it up and throw it away. She
opted for putting it at the bottom of her dresser
drawer. At two in the morning, when Buck finally
settled down, Tessa fell into her bed face-first and
slept the rest of the night fighting fitful dreams
filled with stick figures chasing her around her
locked apartment.

Tessa sat on the edge of her bed the next
morning staring at her clock. Six am. Four hours of
sleep was not enough to be productive. Forty-five
minutes later she was about to leave for work when
she heard a noise outside her apartment door.
Looking through the peephole, she saw Buck
standing in front of her door with his back to it, his
arms crossed over his chest. He looked like a
sentry at a castle gate. A big, intimidating, scream-
all-night-and-make-her-lose-sleep kind of sentry.
Tessa took a long drink from her coffee-filled
travel mug. She didn't have the energy to deal with

the beast blocking her doorway so she waited, checking the peephole every few minutes until Buck finally left. Then she began another day and headed to work so she could yawn and drink coffee for the next eight hours.

Still, each night Tessa couldn't wait to get home from work to her cute little apartment. She checked in on Betty and took long walks on the weekends around the park nearby. And of course, her favorite activity took place in her apartment's big kitchen, where she baked batch after batch of cookies. Tessa was a cookie-baking aficionado. Making a batch of cookies put her in her Zen place.

Yet, by the second week of living in her apartment, very few feelings of Zen could be achieved. Tessa had come to see Buck as more than just slow, or odd. The second week, Tessa realized Buck could be dangerous.

It had been another long day at work. Traffic was beyond intolerable and all she wanted was to put on her sweats, have a Diet Pepsi, and collapse in a chair. Just as she closed the door behind her, however, she realized she'd left her cell phone in the car. She ran back out to get it, but as she came back into the building and started up the stairs, Tessa could see her apartment door standing open. Her mind raced as she crept up the stairs. She didn't think she had left the door open, but she also realized she hadn't locked it. *Idiot.* Arriving at the top of the stairs, she stood in the doorway of her apartment. Buck sat in the big brown chair by the window, as though he'd been patiently waiting for her.

He lolled back in the chair with a smirk on his normally vacant face. One ankle rested on the other knee, his foot twitching.

"Hey Tessa," His voice rumbled. "Thought I'd stop by for a visit." Grinning, he reached up and stroked his beard as he waited for her response.

Tessa stood frozen in the doorway, her legs shaking, and her palms sweating. It's the most she'd ever heard Buck say and she decided she liked him better when he didn't talk so much.

"You came into my apartment when I wasn't here?" The hair on her arms prickled. Her breath came out in a shudder and she wasn't sure if it was because she was frightened or furious. The expression on his face told her yelling at him in anger would not be a good idea. Confrontation seemed to be what he was looking for.

"I figured you'd be right back. I was watching you through my window." He smiled, his mustache twitching. "I like to watch you, Tessa. Did you know that?"

Tessa felt sweat break out on her forehead and she realized her fist was in a tight ball. *You watch me?* As she stood their shaking with anger and fear, many things went through her mind. She wanted to tell him how hard she had worked to move to the city all by herself. She wanted to scream at him for ruining her sleep and frightening her when all she was doing was minding her own business. And at this moment, she wanted to tell him to get the hell out of her apartment. Instead, she kept her mouth tightly pursed.

Buck clearly had mood swings...maybe he was even schizophrenic. He could have been yelling at himself at night. Who knew what was going on in his big freaky head of his? For all she knew he could be the Ted Bundy of St. Louis, and she was his next victim. *Stop it, Tessa. Stop it.*

He chuckled to himself, seemingly amused with her silence. Then he stood, and came up to her with long heavy steps. He stopped just inches from her...close enough she could smell something odd. Not just body odor as much as smoke or incense.

"See you soon, Tessa," he said, then he brushed his arm with hers and slowly descended the stairs.

Tessa's hands shook as she shut herself inside her apartment and locked the door behind her. All of her instincts were screaming this guy was bad news, but common sense told her she was blowing things way out of proportion. Was the guy two bricks short of a load? Clearly. Did he maybe have an extra personality that came out to play on occasion? Possibly. Should her heart be racing a hundred miles an hour? That was the question. Trust your gut or put your big girl panties on and deal. Regardless of whether her feelings were right or wrong, that night she went to Menards and purchased an additional dead bolt for her door. But to lock out the worry about Buck Fischer, she was going to need a friend.

"Julie?" Tessa tried to sound nonchalant. She could hardly blurt out, *I've got a creepy neighbor; can you come over and hang out with me?*

"Hey Tessa." Tessa had met Julie in her Pilates class. She was a perky upbeat kinda gal and that's just what Tessa needed right now.

"Want to come over and bake cookies and drink some wine?" Tessa didn't have to wait long for an answer.

"Be right there!"

About a half hour later, Julie arrived and before long they were up to their elbows in flour and butter as they stirred up a special batch of Chocolate Chip Krispy cookies, Tessa's favorite recipe.

"So, Julie, can you hang out until around midnight?" Tessa licked the cookie dough from her fingers, hoping Julie would be willing.

"Midnight? That's kinda late. I have to work in the morning." Julie dug out a mound of cookie dough with an ice cream scoop and plopped it on the cookie sheet. "Why do you want me to stay so late?"

"I want to know if I'm going crazy or not." Tessa ventured, acting silly, trying to hide her worry.

Tessa hated whiners. She was not the kind of girl who needed rescuing. Tessa had moved away from her small town and loving family with something to prove – that she could do this big city girl thing. The last thing she wanted was her parents, relatives, or friends thinking she was frightened, so up until now, she hadn't mentioned it to anyone. But when Buck blatantly came into her apartment uninvited and acted so odd, well, maybe it was time to 'fess up she was feeling scared.

"Oh, you're crazy alright," Julie grinned. "Seriously, what's going on?" She put the scoop down to listen.

"I have this neighbor downstairs and he gives me the creeps. He came into my apartment today uninvited." Julie's eyes widened. "To be fair, I left the door unlocked." Tessa had no idea why she was making excuses for Buck.

"What do you mean, came in uninvited?" Julie raised an eyebrow.

"Like, I left for a minute without locking the door and when I got back he was sitting in my apartment." Tessa began to chew on her nail. It sounded horrible when she said it out loud.

"Tessa. That's not ok. Have you talked to the apartment manager about that?" Julie put her fists

143

on her hips. "That's pretty serious. Technically, it's breaking and entering."

"No, I don't want to make a big deal out of it. He's a big weird guy and the last thing I need to do is piss him off. Plus, I don't want to be a pest – you know, that person who's always calling the apartment manager complaining about something." *Yeah, right, Tessa. You just keep putting on the brave face. That's working for ya.* "You really think I should talk to the manager." Tessa hated the idea of tattling on her neighbor, but maybe Julie had a point.

"Uh, yeah, Tess. You totally have to tell your manager." Julie rolled her eyes and went back to scooping cookie dough. "But what does me staying till midnight have to do with anything?"

"Oh, I just enjoy your company." Tessa chickened out. She didn't need to make her problems Julie's problems. That wasn't cool. She'd talk to the apartment manager tomorrow like Julie suggested. That was enough. No need to make her hang out and subject her to Buck's screaming.

Julie grinned. "I'm flattered, but seriously, I get up at five. I need to be in bed by eleven. You understand, don't you?"

Tessa understood. She understood she'd be having another sleepless night.

Tessa kept starting new conversations, trying to keep Julie there at least until the screaming started, but Buck was oddly silent that night. Julie finally excused herself around ten thirty and as Tessa expected, his rants began around ten forty-five. *Of course.*

Tessa got ready for bed, determined to take some kind of action the next day. Maybe she would talk to the manager. Maybe she'd talk to the med student across the hall, too. She'd buy herself some earplugs…start drinking a glass of wine before bed… have a turkey sandwich with a glass of warm milk…anything to help her sleep through Buck's yelling.

She stared at herself in the mirror the next morning. Lack of sleep did not look good on her. The dark circles under her eyes were as haunting as her troubled dreams. "Earplugs, Tessa. Go buy earplugs," she said to her reflection.

Around seven am, Tessa heard the front door of the building clunk shut and she knew it would be one of two people leaving; the med student who lived across the hall upstairs, or Buck. Betty rarely left the building. Tessa peeked through the curtains of her second floor window. It was him. She exhaled with heavy relief and then watched him lumber to his truck and drive away. Tessa always waited until Buck left in the morning before she headed out the door herself. No need to run into the big guy. Now that he had left, she grabbed a plate of cookies she and Julie made last night and snatched up her purse. She was going to be late again. She hustled out her front door, locked it up tight, then beat out a quick rhythm on the wooden stairs as she hurried down to apartment two.

"Betty?" Tessa called out and knocked. Betty wouldn't answer until she heard Tessa's voice.

All of the deadbolts slid and the chain lock rattled as it unlatched, then the door cracked open. "Is he gone?" Betty's wide, fear-filled eyes stared through thick, dirty glasses. The small woman got on her tiptoes to look behind Tessa to make sure the hall was clear.

"Yes, I'm sure he's gone. Now let me in." Tessa needed to get going. "I have your cookies for you." She showed Betty the plate.

"Oh, good." Betty opened the door allowing Tessa in, then she huffed at the closed door of Buck's apartment, and slammed her own door shut and locked it up tight. "Chocolate Chip Krispies, or oatmeal raisin today?" Betty chirped as she hurried over to the kitchen counter.

"Chocolate Chip Krispies." Tessa unwrapped the cookies and Betty snatched one up. Tessa smiled and reached over to gently lift the glasses from Betty's face so she could clean them for her as she did every morning. Betty smiled as cookie crumbs fell onto her brightly colored housedress.

"I don't know what I'd do without you, dear." Betty mumbled around her mouthful of cookie, then grabbed another one from the plate.

146

"You'd eat a lot fewer cookies, I would think."
Tessa put the glasses back on Betty's wrinkled
nose. "I have to go. I'm going to be late." Tessa
gave Betty a peck on the cheek. "You need me to
pick anything up for you at the store after work?"
Tessa was already out the door and in the hallway,
her hand ready to shut Betty's door.

"How 'bout a new tabloid magazine," Betty
said as she turned to look back at Tessa, but her
expression quickly changed from joy to dread.
Melted chocolate chips stained her mouth, which
now hung open. Tessa could see fear quite clearly
through the older woman's now-clean glasses, and
that could only mean one thing. The door to the
building clunked shut and Tessa could sense an
imposing presence behind her…hear his heavy
breath.

Betty shuffled as quickly as she could to the
door and pushed it closed, leaving Tessa in the hall
to fend for herself. The locks sounded off with a
speed surprising for Betty's old, arthritic hands.

Tessa's heart accelerated and she tried to
control her breathing as she turned to face the
downstairs neighbor she thought had left for the
day. Buck.

"What are you doing back? I thought you'd left
for the day." Tessa forced a smile and tried to
sound pleasant, but her voice quivered. Her fingers
gripped her purse tightly to keep her hands from

shaking. She glanced out the window of the door. Freedom was just a few feet away.

Buck stepped closer to Tessa. He leaned down from his towering height and inhaled her like she was a plate of food set before him. Tessa knew Betty was watching through the peephole and was most likely shaking in her fuzzy yellow bedroom slippers.

"You make me cookies?" His low voice grumbled out from under his dirty mustache. Foul, damp breath poured from him, hitting her face with a fetid breeze. One of his eyes stared down at her and his other seemed to keep watch on something just off to the left. Tessa wanted to cover her nose, throw up, run screaming from the building, or pass out. Any option would have been better than standing there with Buck. She offered another tight smile. There was just no way around it. Buck Fischer gave her the heebie jeebies.

"I did make a few extra. Do you want them?" She forced herself to look up into the eye focused on her. He nodded. Good old silent Buck was back, it seemed.

She inched around his massive form, trying to hold her breath so she didn't smell any more of him than she had to. "Stay here. I'll be right back." *And please don't follow me.*

She ran up the stairs hoping her small light frame could run faster than his immense one, should he follow. As she worked as fast as she could to unlock her door, she chastised herself for assuming the worst about the man, but how could she not? But still, this paranoia was taking over. She ran into her apartment, grabbed the last four cookies, wrapped them in a paper towel, and hurried back out, locking the door behind her and running back downstairs.

"Here." She panted, out of breath as she handed them to him. She tried to stay at arm's length, but when he took the cookies, he grabbed her arm with his other hand. Her whole body tensed as she stared at the large dirty hand enclosed around her upper arm. He smiled a crooked smile, his dirty yellow teeth bared.

Tessa couldn't take it. She totally flipped out. Jerking her arm away, she tore out of the front door of the building like a frightened animal.

She bolted toward her car, afraid to look behind her for fear he was following her. She struggled to get control of herself. No sleep. Him yelling. Betty warning her. Julie telling her to talk to the apartment manager. It was all piling up like a load of rocks raining down on her. As she drove away, Tessa looked down at her arm where he'd held her and started to cry at the sight of his greasy fingerprints on her blouse. And she had completely forgotten to go talk to the manager.

Stolen Cookies

Tessa always started her day with a visit to Betty. Tessa was fairly sure she was the only company Betty ever received. Visiting her each morning made Betty smile and Tessa liked starting her day with one of Betty's smiles. It made both of them feel good.

Until the next morning when Betty didn't answer her door.

Tessa knocked and knocked, and called out several times, but no answer came. She tried the door and found it unlocked. She felt her heart thump in her chest. Betty's door was always locked. She held her breath. Something was wrong. Tessa crept through the doorway, afraid of what she would find. *No.* There was Betty, sprawled out on the floor, her glasses askew, and her slippers barely clinging to her feet. Tessa closed her eyes to shut out the ugliness and screamed.

Tessa dropped the plate of cookies. Her friend…her defenseless friend. "Oh, Betty." She ran and knelt beside her. Betty lay unconscious with a twisted grimace on her face, but when Tessa put her shaking fingers to Betty's neck she felt a faint pulse. "Hold on, Betty. Hold on." Tessa clutched her cell phone as she called 911, then held Betty's hand, and prayed while she waited for police and an ambulance to arrive. From the hall, she heard the entry door clunk shut, and she saw the cookies she had dropped were now gone.

Tessa's stomach tightened. *Buck.*

The ambulance arrived. As Tessa watched through watery eyes, Betty was hooked up to oxygen and taken away on a stretcher.

"It looks as though Mrs. Sanderson had a heart attack. Do you have any information about her family?" the police officer asked. He had powdered sugar on his black shirt. Myth busted. They do eat donuts.

"I don't think she has any..." Tessa hesitated and blew her nose into a tissue. She looked toward Buck's door.

"Miss Arlington, is there something more you want to tell us?" The officer searched Tessa's eyes.

"Well, her door was unlocked. Betty was afraid of the neighbor across the hall. Buck Fischer. I'm just worried he frightened her and gave her a heart attack." Tessa hated to point a finger, but it was true. She wasn't lying. Betty had been afraid of Buck.

"We can question him, but at Mrs. Sanderson's age, a heart attack isn't unusual."

"I'm sure you're right," Tessa mumbled...but she wasn't sure. She wasn't sure at all.

Tessa finally went to work, but her day was a mess. She cried off and on at the thought of Betty lying there on that floor. Poor thing. Tessa squeezed her eyes shut and tried to force the worry from her brain. After work she went to see Betty in the hospital, but they told her Betty was not allowed visitors yet. "What's wrong?" Tessa asked.

"Are you family?" the nurse questioned.

"No, but…" Tessa didn't get to finish her sentence.

"Only family." The nurse turned and left.

Tessa watched her walk down the hall and felt helpless, but there wasn't much more she could do.

She got home that night to find the apartment manager gone for the day. Confronting her issues about Buck was going to have to wait yet another day. She tried to avoid looking at Betty's door as she ran up the stairs to an apartment that no longer offered peace and quiet, or comfort and tranquility.

The Yelling Continues

Tessa sat on her couch that night searching the apartment listings while watching out her window, listening for the sound of Buck's comings and goings. The clunk of the entry door sent her scurrying to her window…breathing a sigh of relief if it was him leaving…chilling her to the bone when she heard him return. She suspected there was little chance she'd get any sleep tonight what with thinking about Betty.

She found herself alternating between creating scenarios of what would happen if someone broke into her apartment and thinking of why Betty's old heart failed her. Was she attacked? Did Buck break in and scare her within an inch of her life? The questions swirled around her mind endlessly, making it impossible to think straight. She needed to talk to Betty. She needed to know if Buck had done anything to her.

Before, Buck's night terrors kept her pacing, but at least she could sleep once he quieted. Now she didn't know how she would ever sleep soundly again. Every creak of the stairs made her freeze in her steps. She finally decided to try to sleep on the couch with a baseball bat lying on the floor beside her, staring at her doorknob, sure someone was going to try to break in.

Around one in the morning, when Buck had seemed to reach an apex in his yelling, Tessa thought about making cookies. That usually calmed her down. But cookies only reminded her of Betty and when she thought of Betty, all she could think about was the horrible look on Betty's pale face and her tears returned.

This beautiful little apartment she was sure would be the place she could call home for many years had become a place she dreaded being. She wanted out, but couldn't leave. The thought of moving again exhausted her, not to mention a one-year lease looming over her head. Besides, finding a better place wasn't easy. Tessa just wanted to settle where the neighborhood was safe and the rent was affordable. She thought she had found it. But the more she thought about it, the more she came to realize Buck had actually ruined the prospect of her having a happy home. He'd turned the feeling of safety into fear and dread. Hell, he'd even taken away her greatest joy…she hardly even enjoyed baking cookies, for crying out loud.

Tessa looked around her sty of an apartment in disgust. Sleepless nights and long days at work left her with so little energy, she couldn't even remember the last time she had bothered to clean. She had become someone she didn't have much respect for. This time, she would do something. This time, she would take control.

"I want to make a complaint." Tessa stood tall in front of the apartment manager's desk the next morning.

"About?" The woman didn't even look up at Tessa. She was leafing through applications and simultaneously checking her smart phone.

"About Buck Fischer in apartment one, building three." Tessa watched the manager punching in a phone number and then hold up one finger signaling Tessa to wait.

"I'm in a hurry," Tessa tried to sound authoritative but it came out weak.

"Hold on, I need to check my messages," her finger still up. She laid down the phone, jotted down a few notes, then finally gave Tessa a moment of impatient attention.

"Every person, including you, has had a criminal check run before their application is accepted. Buck Fischer, I assure you, passed that test and has no criminal record. I talked to the police yesterday. I'm sorry about Betty's heart attack. I assume you're upset about that. But I doubt Buck had anything to do with that." She stood, scooped up the pile of papers on her desk, straightened them, and started to leave.

"I'm not so sure you're right." Tessa had started chewing on her nails again. "Besides, he yells." The comment sounded like a whimper.

"He what?" The manager stared over her glasses at Tessa.

"Yells. Every night for hours. And one time he came into my apartment uninvited." Tessa tried to stand up straight again.

"When?"

"A few weeks ago." Tessa looked down, embarrassed she hadn't reported it at the time.

"If you would have told me then, I would have talked to him. What happened when you asked him to leave?" The manager looked at Tessa. It seemed as though she might give Tessa her due.

Tessa swallowed hard. "He left." She felt like a nincompoop…a whiney little fool. "But, he was intimidating. Then he drew me this weird picture…and when I found Betty, I'm sure he took the cookies I had made for her." It seemed as if all of what she was going to say would surely be the final nail in his coffin, but even as the words came out of her mouth, they all sounded inane. She was tattling on her neighbor for taking cookies and for drawing a picture.

The manager stared at Tessa for a while then forced a smile that was more sarcastic than sincere. "Hon, he pays his rent on time and no one else has ever complained about him. What do you want me to do?" The manager shrugged her hunched shoulders. "I'm an apartment manager. Not a babysitter. Just avoid him. And if he ever goes into your apartment uninvited and won't leave…then you should definitely give me a call." She exited, held the door, and waited for Tessa to follow her.

As she locked up the office she said over her shoulder, "You from a small town?"

Tessa grimaced. "Yes."

"This is the city, Hon. People yell. It's part of apartment living. You'll get used to it, kid." Then she patted Tessa on the back and hurried down the sidewalk, her papers clutched in her red-nailed hands.

Tessa watched her march away like a little robot, off to ignore someone else's complaints. *Thanks for nothin'.*

She left for work knowing she was going to be late…again. She was still determined to figure out how to resolve her situation. She couldn't continue to live like this. And if the manager wasn't going to help her, she'd just have to help herself.

But by the end of a long day of work, Tessa was exhausted. All of the positive energy she convinced herself she was going to have had evaporated like steam from a cup. By the middle of the night, she was back to pacing, worrying, and wondering how she could possibly continue to stay in this place and she still had no clue how to fix her situation.

By midnight, after two hours of Buck screaming, Tessa was once again tense, sitting in her bed, hugging her pillow, phone in her hand with 911 punched in, ready to hit send. The longer he yelled, the more she thought about how much she desperately needed to sleep, and the more she convinced herself Buck had to have attacked Betty and caused her heart attack.

The next morning Tessa was determined to make the manager listen. She stormed into the office with the courage of her convictions.

The manager, without even looking up from her deskwork, handed Tessa a complaint form. Tessa filled in the form with angry scribbles then threw it on the manager's desk, adding to the pile of other papers from other discontent apartment dwellers. She marched back to her apartment and knocked on the door of her neighbor across the hall. She'd never actually talked to her, but Betty had told her she was a med student...very serious...kept late hours studying. The door opened to a young woman with her nose in a thick book. She stared at Tessa with a question on her face but offered no greeting.

"Hi." Tessa started. "I'm your neighbor across the hall, Tessa Arlington."

"Yes. I've seen you." She clearly wasn't in the mood to chat. She began to tap her pencil on her book and offered an impatient smile.

"Do you have a minute?" Tessa asked. She wanted to be polite, but the impatience of everyone she was dealing with was making it difficult.

"Not really. I'm cramming for a test this afternoon. Some other time, maybe." The neighbor began to shut the door, but Tessa reached out to put her hand on it. The neighbor glared.

"Sorry," Tessa said, "but I was wondering if Buck's yelling was bothering you, too?" Tessa pointed downstairs to Buck's apartment door as she asked.

The woman looked toward Buck's door and shrugged.

"Sorta. Yeah. But a lot of things bother me. I just don't get involved. It's no big deal – this place is a nice location and the rent is affordable so I just turn up my stereo and put my ear buds in. I usually study until about two anyway." She resumed shutting her door.

"Wait," Tessa kept her hand on the door, in spite of the pursed lips and hard eyed glare of her neighbor. "You really don't care?" She found it hard to believe. How could Buck's yelling not bother her? "Has he ever tried to get into your apartment? Or given you a picture he drew? Don't you find him intimidating?"

The med student glared at Tessa. "Actually, right now, it's you I'm finding to be a problem. I have about an hour to study for this test and you're taking up my valuable time." The silence between them hung like a threat.

159

Tessa removed her hand but didn't know what to say. It was irrelevant. The door closed in her face and Miss All Important Med Student would never hear whatever she might have decided to say.

Tessa would have to turn to the police next time things got unpleasant. But she didn't want to be an anonymous phone call at one in the morning. She wanted the precinct to put a face with the grievance and take it seriously. Maybe what she needed to do was go down Saturday morning to file a formal complaint.

First, daunting as it felt, she planned to screw up her courage and talk to Buck.

That was her second mistake.

Tessa brought her shaking hand up to knock on Buck Fischer's door. It was the best day to do this. New neighbors were moving into Betty's old apartment, as her heart attack had been severe enough to keep her in the hospital for an extended time. Betty thought she'd have to move to a nursing home, so she let the apartment go to save money. People coming in and out meant safety in numbers, Tessa thought. Her fist hesitated before she knocked on Buck's door, but she mustered her resolve and gave the wood three good hard raps, then held her breath.

No locks sounded. Not surprising. Why would the big scary man need locks? The door opened a little and through the fissure, she saw Buck's one good eye staring at her.

"Buck, I need to talk to you." Tessa tried to make her voice sound authoritative but it came out shaky.

Buck didn't say a word, but he didn't close the door either.

"Well," she took a deep breath," I have a problem. You yell every night and I'm not getting any sleep. It scares me, too." Tessa blurted out her thoughts. He said nothing. "I'm going to go to the police, Buck. I'm going to file a report." Surely, he'd have something to say to that.

The door slammed shut. Tessa heard shuffling inside, then the door opened just enough for Buck to emerge into the hallway. Tessa backed up. He loomed above her, and he looked pissed.

"You don't want to do that. That would be bad," Buck said in a steady voice as he stared at her with both eyes now. She began to shake, but held her ground. She *would* go to the police. She had to.

The new neighbor walked into the entryway, said hello, and stopped in surprise to stare at the obvious confrontation. Tessa didn't turn to look at him or return a hello. She kept her eyes on Buck, fixed in his intimidating glare.

The neighbor shrugged at the lack of response, then shuffled into his apartment and locked the door.

Great, Tessa thought. So much for safety in numbers.

"Well, I'm going to do it, Buck. I don't know why, but you scream until all hours and it's not ok. You have to stop it. I can't take it anymore." Her eyes welled up with tears. "Why? Why are you screaming and yelling all night?" She was about to crack. This confrontation was too intense. She didn't like arguments and this was the worst she'd ever had.

"I scream?" He said, his mouth twitching with a little smile. "Are you sure about that?" He taunted her. "How 'bout I tell you I'll try to stop." Buck tilted his head and the corner of his mouth pulled into a teasing grin. "How 'bout that, Tessa?"

She hadn't been prepared for him to give her any feedback. In her imagination, she was going to lay down the law and storm away. Buck usually never said a word, aside from the time he'd been in her apartment that one day. His response threw her off. She crossed her arms over her chest and finally looked away. A tear rolled down her cheek and she swiped at it, angry to show her fear.

"One more night, Buck. If you can't quit the yelling, tonight I will call the cops and report it. You've been warned." Tessa hoped he was good for his word because she was truly at her wit's end.

The night came and the yelling began. Now Tessa regretted not going to the police during the light of day. Everything seemed so much more horrible at night. She was exhausted and frightened, but damn it, she said she'd report him and that was exactly what she was going to do.

She picked up the phone and made the call. "I want to report a disturbance. There is a man screaming at the top of his lungs in the apartment below me. He sounds dangerous."

Tessa chewed her nails as she watched through her window, waiting for the police to arrive. Buck was still screaming up a storm in the apartment below her. As the police pulled up and began to walk toward the apartment building, Tessa began to fill with hope. Someone was finally taking her seriously. Someone was going to help her.

Then Buck became silent. He must have seen them, too. Tessa heard the knock on Buck's door downstairs. She didn't know if she should go out in the hall or stay locked in her apartment. After a few minutes, a knock came to her door. She swallowed hard then opened it enough to see the officer standing there. "Yes?" she said through the crack.

"I'm here about the disturbance you called in." The officer said without inflection.

"Yes?" Tessa didn't know what to do. She'd never done anything like this before. She felt like she was in trouble.

"I've visited with the resident of apartment one and he didn't understand the complaint. He said he was sleeping and I woke him. He looked as though he had just woken up, Ma'am. He was not yelling when I arrived on the premise." The officer waited, staring at Tessa through the crack of her door.

"He was right before you came. Yelling, that is. He quit just as you were walking up." Tessa's voice was weak and pleading as she began to wonder how she could prove she lived above a lunatic.

"All I can do is let you know I have responded to your complaint and tell you I have addressed the situation with your neighbor. I advise you consider purchasing earplugs." Then the officer smiled ever so slightly, turned and left.

Earplugs? Seriously? That was the advice of law enforcement? She shut the door then wandered in a daze to the window to watch the officer drive away. Buck's yells began within seconds of the police car leaving, and every few words she could clearly hear the sound of her name.

Alone

Two more nights went by and each night she called into the police to report a disturbance. Two more times, Buck quieted when the police arrived, and two more times the officer came to her door, each time more irritated with her for calling them out. Each night when the police left, the yelling increased to a decibel surely no one in the building could sleep through. She started hearing specific words. "Tessa, hurt, bitch, kill"…she sat with her back against her apartment door and her hands pressed against her ears. This feeling of helplessness was eating her alive.

Finally, she went across the hall to bang on the med student's door. Buck stopped yelling when he heard Tessa's pounding. The med student came to the door after several minutes of Tessa banging.

"What the hell do you want?" She stood there glaring, in her oversized Rams t-shirt, her hair stuck out in all directions and her ear buds in her hands.

Her neighbor's words pushed Tessa back. "I'm sorry for waking you…but seriously, how can you sleep with all that yelling?"

"We've talked about this. Get some ear buds and quit bothering me!" Her sneer and squinted eyes left Tessa reeling.

"But this is outrageous. Don't tell me you can actually sleep through this." Tessa could feel her temper begin to boil. Normally she would never start an argument, but she had been pushed to her breaking point and hadn't slept well in weeks.

Then she heard the door downstairs open. Buck glared up at her, then slammed his door shut. By the time her attention refocused on the neighbor, her door had closed as well.

Tessa went downstairs, her bare feet quick upon each step. She banged on the door of Betty's old apartment. No one came, but she continued to bang and bang. She had to find someone else who would understand. From upstairs, she heard the med student's apartment door open again, "Just go to bed. You're keeping everyone up!" Just then, the door to apartment two opened. The bleary-eyed man stared at her in disbelief.

"What do you want?" He mumbled as he frowned, rubbing his eyes.

"The yelling. Don't you hear the yelling? Doesn't it bother you?" Tessa's voice had reached a fever pitch.

"Lady, you woke me up. I gotta work in the morning. Are you nuts?" The man scratched the stubble of his beard. "Are you the one who keeps calling the cops? You need to settle down. Yeah, it bugs me, but man, this is the city. People yell."

"Yeah, get a grip," she heard from the med student above. "Did you move here from the country or something? This is apartment living.

People yell, people fight, faucets drip, the heat quits working. Just shut up and deal." The med student was hanging over the railing now. The man in apartment two looked up at the med student. "Yeah," he said in agreement, but he clearly wasn't as awake or ticked off as she was. He turned then said, "Maybe get some ear plugs." Then he shut his door. Tessa heard the med student's door slam, and she was left there in the entryway, wondering if she was losing her mind, or if everyone in the building was crazy.

Make Me Some Cookies

Tessa finally slipped into a troubled sleep. Her dreams were tormented and filled with fight and loss. Her alarm clock blared and she heaved herself up wondering how she would ever get through the day. Bleary eyed, she drifted from room to room, one thing after another going wrong. The shower water never became hot enough. The toilet paper ran out. She had to dig a pair of slacks out of the laundry. She could only find one of the shoes she wanted to wear, which made her cry thinking of Betty's fuzzy slippers. No coffee left in the can. No butter for her toast. She'd been so upset lately she hadn't been thinking clearly. She hadn't been taking care of her apartment or herself. She looked around. The place was a pit. Dirty clothes were strewn about her bedroom, the towels in the bathroom hadn't been washed in weeks, and her sheets hadn't either. Her fridge was bare and the sink was full of dirty dishes. She looked at herself in the mirror by the door, as she was about to leave for work.

No. She couldn't do it. She decided to change into jeans and a t-shirt and call in sick. She *was* sick. Sick of her life, sick of her situation, and sick of feeling like she was losing her grip. She needed to clean her apartment, get groceries, take a good long nap, and just be herself...normal...calm and happy Tessa. She could barely remember what it felt like to feel rested and calm. And it was time to buy some ear plugs.

Tessa began to clear the dishes from the sink so she could wash them up. She ran the water and scrubbed at the sink, but the water wouldn't go down the drain. *Great.* The drain was plugged. She grabbed her purse and headed out to buy some drain cleaner and groceries. She would bring her life and her apartment back to the pretty, little place she had wanted it to be. She would learn how to toughen up and be a city dweller, an apartment person. She'd be someone who could sleep right through screams, someone who minded their own business, someone who could survive.

Although exhausted, Tessa worked her day away and by mid-afternoon, her apartment sparkled, and she had a big container filled with homemade cookie dough waiting in the fridge. She was feeling more like her old self. She could reclaim her life. She would not lose who she was to the likes of Buck Fischer, no matter how much he scared her.

At three in the afternoon, she baked a dozen cookies. One for her, as usual, then she put four to a plate and left one plate in front of the doors of the new neighbor downstairs and the med student across from her. Cookies could fix anything and right now she needed friends, not enemies.

"You make cookies for me?" Buck stood staring at her from the doorway of his apartment. He looked sad...regretful, maybe.

"No, Buck. I'm sorry. If you quit screaming every night, I promise to bring you cookies every morning. But right now, you don't deserve them." Tessa couldn't believe she said the confrontational words. It sounded like something her mother would have told her. Maybe that's what was needed here, though. Buck was so child-like sometimes. A scolding might be just what was called for.

"I don't yell. I work all night." Buck's face dropped. "I want you to be my friend." It looked as though he might break into tears.

Tessa frowned in confusion. One moment he was screaming obscenities and the next moment he sounded like a little boy.

"I can't be your friend until you stop screaming at night." Tessa didn't wait for Buck's reaction. She turned and scampered up the stairs and into her apartment, locking the door behind her.

The confrontation with Buck confused her, but by the time she cleaned up the kitchen again, exhaustion finally overtook her. She lay down on her couch and slipped into a deep, drooling sleep.

When she woke, she jolted from the couch and made a wide-eyed search of the dark room. *How long did I sleep?* Then the knock that must have jarred her awake, came again. Quiet, but loud enough for her to startle. *What time is it?* She stumbled from the couch, sure her ears were tricking her. Maybe she was still dreaming. She checked the clock on the microwave. One in the morning. The knock came again – louder this time. She pushed back her hair and took a deep breath. She had to wake up. *I slept nine hours.* Then his voice came like a muffled threat through the timber of her doorway.

"Tessa? I know you're in there."

She wasn't dreaming. She ran with light footfalls to the door to peek out the peephole. Buck grinned wildly in fisheye-fashion on the other side. She jerked back, alarmed at the sight of him. She inched back from the door and as quietly as she could, she picked up a chair from the kitchen table and propped it under the knob of the door. She found her phone and stood there, shaking in fear as she called the police.

"Bye, Tessa. Sleep well. This is your last night unless you make me some cookies," she heard Buck say, and then the heavy footsteps of Buck Fischer went down the stairs, and the door ca-chunked as he left the building.

"St. Louis Police Department," the dispatcher droned in her ear.

"Never mind. False alarm," Tessa answered in defeat. They wouldn't do anything anyway. This was it. She was wide-awake now and she had tolerated all she could. Her mind was clear and she would be damned if the likes of Buck Fischer continued to ruin her life.

Time to Do Some Baking

The idea hit her like a bolt of lightning. Everything became terribly apparent. She would have to take matters into her own hands.

Tessa turned on her oven. It was time to do some down and dirty baking. She would make a special batch of cookies for Buck Fischer. Something to get rid of him for good. She'd make that jerk pay. He ruined her life…her happy little, cookie-baking, simple, routine life. Damn him. And she was sure he had something to do with Betty's heart attack. Betty had been the only kind neighbor Tessa had and the poor old thing didn't deserve to live like a frightened rabbit buried in a hole. And neither did she. Tessa was fed up. All she wanted was to be nice to people and go to work and be a good, quiet neighbor who helped people out. She didn't play her music loud. She'd always been a good daughter, a good student, and a good employee. She had always tried hard to do everything right. Why was she being punished? She knew people who had wild parties at their apartments. They trashed furniture, busted holes in walls, ruined carpets, tore drapes, and even set things on fire. Not her. No! She was always the respectable girl. Well, fat lot of good it did her to behave. No more.

She hefted the big bowl of cookie dough from the fridge and got out her cookie sheets. She made two batches – one for the neighbors and for friends at work and the other sheet? All for Buck. She smiled as she reached down beneath the sink to get the drain cleaner. Tessa smiled a half-insane-from-worry smile. He could eat the whole damn batch as far as she cared.

After she baked off the first batch, cleaned up the pans, and put the cookies away in the cupboard, she then put parchment paper on the second pan and began to mix the drain cleaner into the last batch of cookie dough. She'd clean his pipes alright. He was all clogged up with evil and she was determined to get it out…all out! The apartment smelled a little funny as the cookies baked. While she waited, she packaged up the other cookies and labeled them clearly so she knew which cookies were which.

When she pulled the poisoned cookies from the oven she stood over them and laughed until she cried.

Damn it.

What had she been reduced to? How could she have possibly gone this far? Had she lost her ever-lovin' mind? That lunatic downstairs had pushed her right over the edge. She took the cookies and dumped them into the trashcan. No way could she stoop so low. Now she would spend the rest of her life trying to forget she even baked them in the first place. She trudged to her bedroom, threw herself on the bed, and sobbed herself to sleep. But sleep didn't last very long. Within the hour, a loud noise woke her with a jolt. The time for quiet knocking was apparently over. Buck now hammered on her door with angry fists.

"I smell. cookies Tessa. The big bad Buck is here and I'm gonna blow your house down for those cookies!"

Tessa screamed and lurched from her bed. She ran to the front room and saw the doorknob turning and the wood of the door bowing in under Buck's weight. So far, the locks held, as did the chair. She grabbed her phone and dialed the police with frantic shaking fingers. "Help, my neighbor is trying to break into my apartment."

His body slammed into her door. "Tessa? You're not being a bad girl and calling those cops again are you?" He yelled as his fists continued to beat on the door. The lock busted and wood splintered into the room and the door cracked open.

Her screams pierced the air like a siren. She shoved herself against the door, pushing back as hard as she could. She had dropped the phone and could only hear the faint voice of the dispatcher saying,

"Hello? Hello? Ma'am, are you still there?"

Tessa screamed, "Help! This is Tessa Arlington in apartment three..." then Buck heaved himself at the door, his impact throwing Tessa to the floor. She scrambled to her feet and hurried back, trying to put her weight into her efforts, but she wasn't big enough...wasn't strong enough. His arm came through the crack of the now open door and he reached for the chair to dislodge it. "Help!"

Tessa screamed, hoping the dispatcher was still on the line. "263 Brant Street, Lafayette Square." *Dear God let her have heard me.* Buck's hand grabbed the chair and pulled it away then she heard a grunt as he slammed himself into the door. All three chains busted and the door flew open wide.

Tessa fell to the floor, but scrambled up immediately even as she screamed and screamed until her throat felt raw. Once she found her footing she started to run, but he was too close, his hand grabbed her from behind. He spun her around to face him.

"Now, what kind of hostess are you, Tessa? You should offer me milk and cookies!" He roared at her, spit hitting her face, his hands squeezing the blood from her upper arms.

Tessa pulled and pulled but he only laughed.

"I smell cookies," he said, now dragging her toward her kitchen. "I know you were baking. The whole damn apartment building knows you were baking. Now tell me where the stinking cookies are!" His roar shook her and she had no remorse when she told him,

"I threw them away. They're in the garbage. Go have as many as you want, you sick freak." Despite her fear and racing heart, she sneered at the monster holding her in a death grip. Anger glowed in her eyes and she hoped like hell he was enough of a pig to eat from the trash.

Buck opened the cupboard under the sink and pulled out the trashcan to see the cookies. "You bitch. You actually threw my cookies away?" He shoved her against the refrigerator. Her back slammed into something she recognized. She'd purchased a corkscrew on a magnet. She reached behind with her hand and grabbed it, flipped the corkscrew out and jabbed it into the hand Buck clutched her arm with.

He howled and pulled away, releasing Tessa long enough for her to run to her bedroom, slamming and locking the door behind her. She didn't have much time, he'd break through it without much effort. What could she do? The window? She would jump from the second floor. She ran to the window, but before she could act, she heard footsteps pounding up the stairs. The police, she hoped, but she hadn't heard sirens. It didn't matter. Someone was coming to save her. That's all that mattered.

"No!" She heard Buck yell out. Then something crashed at her bedroom door. In a panic, she ran to her closet and buried herself behind clothes, shoes, and hangers. She shook and cried as she heard fighting and yelling like she'd never heard before. Each thud of bodies sounded like an earthquake. She heard pictures crashing to the ground and furniture being overturned, but she didn't hear the sound of police. Just Buck yelling, as though he was talking to himself. "No, Don't, Stop it," then, "Stay out of it, I'll do what I want, Leave, now!" Tessa strained to listen…a grunt, a fall, silence…then her bedroom door crashed open.

A hesitation, then three heavy footsteps stomped toward the closet she cowered in. The door opened and Buck's big hand, covered in blood, reached in to grab her. This was the end. He would kill her, or worse. She screamed her loudest as Buck pulled her from the closet, and picked her up like a rag doll. Her struggle made him hold her tighter as he carried her out of the bedroom and into the apartment.

As Buck carried her toward the door leading out of the apartment, she saw a man on the floor amidst the overturned trash. Cans of tuna and vegetables, wrappers from meat and cheese, and a dozen tainted cookies lay scattered around him.

Tessa gasped. She looked from Buck to the unconscious man on the floor and she shook her head in disbelief. Was she seeing correctly?

"Twins," she gasped as she looked at Buck to see his eyes filled with tears. He kept plodding along and carried her out of her apartment, down the stairs, and into the breaking dawn. Tessa saw her two neighbors and the apartment manager standing at the curb, ready to greet the police who were skidding to a stop in front of the apartment. Tessa's head swam and the last thing she heard was the med student telling her, "Everything will be ok."

One Month Later

Tessa woke bright and early. The sun danced into her window like a child beckoning her to come and play. She hopped into the shower and scrubbed away the remnants of a great night's sleep. Later, she flitted around her happy little apartment. Everything was back to normal now. Management had puttied and repainted the walls, and replaced the doors and locks. The maintenance man even fixed her clogged drain and put in a garbage disposal, too.

Three plates of cookies sat on her counter. She snitched one for her breakfast and washed it down with a glass of milk. The two other plates she would give to her neighbors. In the end, they really had been there for her in her time of need.

She found out the new neighbor downstairs had called the police and the apartment manager. When the fight broke out, he and the med student heard it and wanted to help, but were afraid. The med student ended up being who looked after Tessa when she passed out that ugly morning. She also checked in on Tessa for a full week after, making sure she was doing all right. A nice gal in the end.

A week after the break-in, the police visited Tessa. After much questioning, Buck had told them all about his brother, Bill, and how Bill had been hiding out in Buck's apartment. They were identical twins – Buck had always been slow…slow enough to be easily manipulated by his brother. Truth be told, Buck needed assistance, but his family didn't have that kind of money, or even care enough to worry about it. It made for a perfect façade for Bill's twisted mind. Bill had moved to St. Louis eight months before. He'd been living in Kansas City prior. One too many sloppy mistakes had the law there looking for him. Living like a shadow with Buck had always been Bill's best escape plan. He'd been manipulating Buck for many years. Bill demanded Buck keep his secrets and if he didn't the consequences were dire. So Buck worked every night at a factory, while his brother stayed home, being his own kind of crazy and doing as many drugs as his brother's income could buy until he decided it was time to move on. No one even knew he was there. Although Buck was slow, Bill was insane in the worst of ways. Turned out this crazy dance in the Fischer family had been going on since they were boys, and Buck was terrified of Bill.

Tessa shivered as she heard the explanation. Poor Buck.

"Right from the moment you moved in, Bill had his eye on you." The woman's police uniform was as official as the somber look on her face. "He had a sick obsession with you and it was all Buck could do to keep you safe." Tessa's stomach dropped. Poor Buck. "Buck missed work once, just to stand guard outside of your apartment so his brother couldn't get to you." Tessa's eyes filled with tears of guilt. If she had only known. "The night Bill broke in, Buck happened to come home early from work. That's where you got lucky." The officer smiled, but her eyes remained serious. Blessed, not lucky, Tessa thought.

"I wish he'd have just told me he had a twin brother." Tessa shook her head, wondering at the twisted hold Bill must have had on Buck.

"Bill told him he couldn't, and Buck had been doing what his brother told him for his entire life." The officer shrugged. "There are a lot of messed up people in this world."

"And you get to meet most of them don't you?" Tessa offered a sympathetic smile.

"It's part of the job." The officer nodded.

* * *

Two batches of cookies came out of the oven, smelling like heaven. Tessa leaned over them and inhaled a big sniff of happiness. Everything was right with her world again, thanks to Buck Fischer and her neighbors.

Quick taps on her neighbor's door bought a smiling face.

"Hey Sara!" Tessa smiled at her med-student neighbor. They were now good friends. Sara had grown up in New York, and was teaching Tessa how to toughen up to city living. Tessa was returning the favor by bringing her a plate of cookies a few times a week.

Then Tessa toddled down to knock on the door of her downstairs neighbor across the hall, Raymond. Before her knuckles hit the wood, the door opened.

"What kind today?" Raymond asked with a broad smile.

"Chocolate walnut." Tessa handed over the little plate. Turned out Raymond was a pretty good guy. He even helped her change a flat tire on her car one morning.

Then on to the last door of the apartment building. Her favorite door. A new tenant had moved in after Buck moved out and they carted Bill off to the hospital, then to jail. Turned out Bill wasn't dead, just incredibly unconscious from a few direct hits to his noggin by Buck. Nothing could have relieved Tessa more. That horrible night, she worried her cookies killed Bill. She was sure by the looks of him he was dead as a doornail. Not the case. But that was all in the past. Life was good again. Things were right. Her apartment was perfect and her neighbors? Well, they couldn't be better.

Three quick raps and the door opened.

"Good morning, Betty!" Tessa was greeted with a big toothy grin and a warm hug.

"How's my girl this morning?" Betty was all moved in. Once Betty had stabilized, Tessa had visited her every day she could. Her heart attack kept her in the hospital for quite some time, but several good things happened from it. A long-lost cousin showed up and one thing led to another…memories led to ideas…and soon, Betty and Maude were roommates, right in the newly-painted and re-carpeted apartment that once belonged to Buck and secretly to Bill Fischer. Turned out Maude was as much of a clean freak as Betty was a hoarder so they kept each other busy, one messing things up, the other cleaning up after her.

"Oatmeal raisin for you and Maude." Tessa peeked around Betty and gave Maude a wave.

Then she was off to visit the Bethesda Group Home. It was a great place where people of varying needs could live and work. It was just where Buck needed to be. He'd been manipulated and abused by his twin brother for his entire life. Now, he could work at the home as a janitor and get the assistance he really needed.

Tessa smiled as she walked with lively steps up the sidewalk to Bethesda. She could see Buck watching out the large window as she walked up the steps of the large porch. She entered the facility and Buck met her with a broad smile.

"Hey, Buck. How are you today?" Tessa gave him a little one-armed hug. Buck didn't really like physical affection but he tolerated hugs from Tessa.

"Ok," he said shyly. Buck sported a nice short haircut and shaved beard these days. It exposed his dimples and revealed a face of innocence.

"Is that a new shirt?" She admired his 3XL plaid collared shirt. "And new pants, too?" She whistled. Buck blushed. He always dressed up for Tessa on Saturday when she visited.

Buck and Tessa sat at a table in the sunshine of the large front window. She told him all about Sara, Raymond, and Maude, and how much Betty liked her new apartment. As Tessa rambled on, filling Buck in about the details of her life, Buck quietly munched away on his plate of cookies and listened with a look of peace on his face. He was happy. Tessa realized she was happy too. She really had found the perfect little apartment, after all.

Hot in the Kitchen

A FOUR-COURSE CONTEST

Bring your best recipe & ingredients

Create a Four-Course Meal with three other teammates

Compete to win

$40,000!

A FOUR-COURSE COMPETITION

Damon Hades had many faces. He moved in every circle and at every time throughout the annals of the world. He once whispered in Pilot's ear, had a persuasive chat with Hitler, and gave a few ideas to Mao, too. But those were some of the highlights of his career. One can't expect to make headlines every day. He was competing with many other professionals in his field, after all.

Damon's normal routine led him to millions of souls across the globe…people on the edge…people contemplating the choice of right or wrong. His job? To tip the scales. Acquire one more soul for his master's dark army. And Damon was good at his job. Very good.

Sheila Nells was a woman he had yet to persuade. Damon wasn't sure she would ever cross over to the dark side, but she *was* a woman of power, money, and influence. He kept close tabs on people like Sheila. He could use them to suit his needs. She probably wasn't up for murder, but for arranging a party that was to die for, Sheila was his go-to gal.

What Sheila responded to most was anything to do with food. While she was a painfully thin woman who survived on toast and martinis, being seen in the right restaurants and knowing the best caterers for fabulous galas was of the utmost importance to Sheila Nells. The woman hob-nobbed with foodies from all over the planet and Damon decided it was time to put a new idea in her elitist head. A cooking competition seemed in order. One funded by the wealthy for the sake of a good cause, like feeding the homeless or providing school lunches for poor children…something in that noble vein. She'd bite that bait like a starving fish in a shallow pond. Then he only needed to wait for her to do what she did best and the stage would be set for a gamble Damon was eager to wager.

Damon had invested time and effort into four different women over the past year…four good cooks. He thought he could easily push them over the edge of good and into the roiling waters of revenge. But three of them were goody two-shoes about the whole thing, and one…well good fates intervened, to a degree at least. Roberta Butler crept closer to the edge of darkness than any of the others. Truly, Lester was one of the finest of the evil minions Damon had ever known. Who could really blame her for wanting to kill the old bastard? Roberta was still stained by her intent but saved in that she was avenging her cousin. But Damon had a strong suspicion she could easily be the one he could count on to reel the others back in to his boat.

One way or the other, it didn't sit right with him. He should have been able to make them all commit crimes that couldn't be forgiven.

One thing Damon knew as fact: evil ran in packs. If he could just get those four women together, all capable of dastardly thoughts and deeds, then he could lure them into his world and win their devotion. He would tempt them with something they never thought they could have and then, surely, he could glean four new souls. It would seem hardly worth the effort to some, but Damon knew that, once, even Attila the Hun was someone's little boy, Vlad the Impaler once cooed for his mother, and Hitler hoped to be a gentle artist. Who knew what these women would be capable of in a group? Collectively, he felt sure they could all raise a little hell. Besides, Damon had always wanted his own little harem.

Now, all he had to do was morph ever so slightly. For Sheila's sake, he would become Hank James, food circuit beefcake, and bartender extraordinaire. It was one of his favorite roles. The new food trenders loved a good Mixologist.

"Sheila, darling!" Hank sauntered into the foyer of Sheila Nell's well-appointed home. Hank went in for a kiss on each cheek as he held her heavily jeweled fingers. "You look fabulous. That color is *so* striking on you!"

Sheila blushed like a schoolgirl. It really didn't take much to wrap her around his finger. He'd plant a few ideas and before long, she'd do his bidding.

"You look delicious yourself," Sheila's eyes traveled up and down his tall, muscular frame. Hey. If a demon could take any shape, why wouldn't he make himself as handsome and sexy as he could?

"Sheila, I have an idea I'd like to run past you. I think you're the only woman I know who could pull this off properly." He squeezed her hand. "It will be a food extravaganza that people will be talking about for a very long time.

Sheila's eyes lit up like crystal in candlelight. Damon…uh, Hank…knew Sheila's weakest link. She wanted, even needed, to be at the very top of the social food chain. He'd throw her that bone, provided it could bring the right handful of young women his way.

Two martinis later Hank and Sheila had agreed on plans. A cooking competition in the heart of America…Warren Buffet's playground…would surely put Sheila's name on the top of culinary event organizers lists. The publicity would be fabulous. All that was left to do was send out the invitations.

"Let me take care of that, Sheila. You've enough to do, and when it comes to picking the right people, I've got quite a knack for it." Hank patted Sheila's hand. She nodded in acceptance of his offer and proposed a toast.

"Here's to a great competition. If they can't take the heat, they should get the hell out of the kitchen!"

THE COMPETITORS

Gloria Davis leaned back in her leather desk chair, her feet propped on her large mahogany desk. It had been Larry's old desk – but it was hers now. Drunk with new power? No, she wouldn't say that. But as she stretched her legs she knew life was good. She wiggled her foot, snuggly fit in her sleek black Kate Spade pumps, as she looked around her professionally-decorated office. The printing on her opaque glass door said *Gloria Davis, Director of Acquisitions*.

Jill popped her head in the door. "Is there anything else you need before I take off for the day?"

Jill was one of the four people who now worked under Gloria. All of her people were top-notch, and all of them were aware how much Gloria appreciated them.

"No, no. I'm good. Hey, how's your little boy? Still fighting that cold?" Gloria asked.

"The sitter just called and said he has a low fever. I'm thinking he might have strep throat." Jill frowned.

Gloria swung her feet off the desk and stood up. "Listen, you take tomorrow off. Be with that boy and take him to the doctor. We'll call if we have any questions." Gloria went over and gave Jill a little hug.

"Really? Oh, Gloria. That means a lot to me." Relief showed in her eyes.

No employee of Gloria's would ever be treated the way Larry Holmquest had treated her.

Jill left and Gloria scooted up to her desk and began to rifle through some of the little piles of papers in front of her. One in particular had been waiting patiently for her attention. She found the red-checkered header at the bottom of the stack and pulled it out.

She flipped the colorful front of the flyer over to read the details of the competition. Omaha. September 12, 13, and 14. $175 entry fee, included meals and accommodations at the Hilton. She tapped her freshly-manicured nails on the desktop. *Why not?* She needed a get-away and she'd always wanted to see how her jalapeño poppers would fare in a competition. They'd certainly done right by her so far in life. The corners of her mouth turned up into a wicked smile and she wrote the check for the competition. After all, it really was a killer recipe.

Roberta Butler hadn't made her potato salad since last summer, but she felt she'd waited long enough. Although her intentions had been nefarious, fate had intervened. The old creeper died from a heart attack induced by his wife. Her hands were clean. She could sleep at night, and she figured Aunt Camilla slept just fine, too.

July was upon her and for the first time she could remember, her mother had only sent a quick email reminder about the annual family picnic. No phone call. No insisting she *had* to come. Roberta politely declined. She was going to the lake with several friends and she couldn't wait.

It was going to be a hot one, she thought, as she put the final touches on her potato salad. She sprinkled chopped green onions on top for garnish, put it in her cooler right beside her strawberry wine coolers, and grabbed her sunscreen. She was due for a wonderful Fourth of July.

As she was about to leave her apartment, Roberta noticed the flyer tacked to the bulletin board she kept by her front door. She had pinned this up last week and had been giving it serious consideration. It was for a cooking competition in Omaha, Nebraska. She could afford it. Hmm. She did make amazing potato salad. Why not? She put the cooler down and quickly made out the check. No time like the present. She was due for an adventure and this seemed right up her alley.

Chicky Torres heard the screen door bang shut. She smiled. Dan was coming in to check on her. She loved that man.

"I'm heading to town. You need anything?" Dan asked as he peeked around the doorway.

"Nope. I'm good." Chicky had her feet up, a fan blowing full-speed on her face, and a tall glass of ice water in her hand.

"You sure? A magazine? Those vinegar chips you like? How 'bout some ice cream and pickles?" He grinned. He knew she couldn't leap to her feet as easily as she would have a few months ago.

"Dan. Darnit. Git!" She slipped her fingers into her glass, plucked out an ice cube, and hurled it across the room. He ducked, then she heard him laughing as he left. He did love to tease her and she loved it when he did.

Chicky rubbed her growing belly. *Good Lord if this kid is as big as his father, childbirth is going to kill me*, she thought.

She actually *was* having a craving. What she wanted, even though it had to be 100 degrees outside, was a big bowl of her chili. She'd taken to mixing in a spoonful of peanut butter to make it even creamier. Dan thought she was crazy to ruin good chili that way, but hey, she was pregnant and she'd eat her chili the way she wanted to.

Chicky wasn't quite to the wobbling stage yet, but she felt like a Weeble. Dan still thought she was all kinds of hot and then some. Grunting, she lifted herself from her cozy chair and shuffled to the kitchen to make a fresh batch of chili.

She dialed the cell phone. "Hey, Dan? I did remember something I need you to pick up." She paused. "No. Not pickles. I need peanut butter." She rolled her eyes. "Yes. I'm making chili again."

Chicky gathered the newspapers and magazines from the kitchen counter so she could spread out and cook. A flyer she'd been shuffling around for a week slipped out and floated to the floor. The big $40,000 begged for her attention. Kneeling, she picked it up. *Why not?* She and Dan needed a little vacay before the baby came. Sure, Omaha wasn't Jamaica or anything, but it would still be a getaway and hey, the Hilton…not too shabby. They were more Super 8 kinda people, so the Hilton would be livin' it up, big time. $175 wasn't much for an entry fee. And $40,000 split four ways…well, ten grand would pay for a real vacation next year. She imagined herself somewhere on a beach with her toes in the sand and a margarita in her hand. Of course, there was no question. Her chili would totally win. After all. It *was* to die for.

Tessa Arlington twisted the ring on her finger. She looked down at the little glimmering diamond and smiled so wide it hurt her cheeks.

"You looking at that engagement ring again?" Jacob sat at the kitchen counter reading a paper while Tessa cleaned up after making a batch of chocolate chip krispy cookies.

"Of course I am. It's beautiful." Her eyes glinted as she leaned across the counter to kiss her fiancé. Then she slid a plate of warm cookies toward him and poured him a glass of ice-cold milk.

It was less than a month after Buck moved out when Tessa met Jacob. He was one of the counselors at Bethesda, where Buck now lived. One kismet meeting and their relationship blossomed. Now they were planning a spring wedding for next year.

"Hey, Tessa, I have an idea." Jacob pulled out a flyer and laid it on the counter for her to see. "I think you should enter this cooking competition in Omaha, Nebraska." He pushed the flyer toward her.

She studied the flyer. "Really? In Nebraska?" She tilted her head and studied Jacob.

"I know. Not the most exotic of places, but the Hilton will be sweet and the entry fee isn't much at all. You *know* you'd win. Your cookies are amazing. Like, melt in your mouth, no one can have just one, circles of love." He shoved an entire cookie in his mouth, then talked around his mouthful, "You know I'm right!" Some cookie fell out onto the counter.

"Jacob!" She laughed and wiped up the mess. "I don't know. This is a national competition. There will be seriously good cooks entered. I don't think so." Tessa turned to put the milk away and from behind, Jacob said, "Too late. I already entered you."

She spun around. "What?" Her mouth hung open, but then she smiled. No one believed in her as much as Jacob. "You know what?" she said to him as she leaned over and grabbed his face.

"Yeah. I know. You love me."

Meet and Greet

Tessa and Jacob emerged from the walkway of the plane and into Eppley Airport, happy about their pleasant flight and ready to get to that swank hotel. Tessa imagined fluffy down pillows and a bed far more comfy than the old twin bed back in her little apartment in St. Louis.

They began to head toward the escalator to go outside and find a cab when Tessa ran right into a pregnant redhead. They both grunted on impact and Tessa bounced backwards, destined for the floor. The redhead's fellow caught her just before she hit the ground. Tessa looked up and for a moment remembered another huge man in her past, but the one keeping her from the airport floor had a nice smile and a worried expression that made her laugh.

"Whoa, there." He said as he easily stood her upright.

"Now don't be man-handling complete strangers, Dan." The redhead said with a laugh. "Sorry 'bout that! We should have been paying attention instead of just chargin' through here like cattle out of a chute."

"No, no, I'm the one who needs to apologize," Tessa pointed to the woman's round belly. "When are you due?"

"The baby is only a month away!" Dan grinned with pride.

"She wasn't asking you!" the redhead jabbed Dan in the arm.

Jacob reached out a hand, "Thanks for catching my gal." He and Dan shook.

"I'm Tessa," Tessa reached out and took the redhead's extended hand. "That's Jacob, my fiancé."

"Chicky Torres. I have a weird name. I know. Chiquita. Like the banana. What's a girl to do?" She shrugged and Tessa grinned in response.

"Well, we'd better keep moving. We have to sign in for a competition." Tessa explained. She was so excited she could barely contain herself.

"Not the cooking competition at the Hilton?" Chicky asked, a grin spreading across her face.

"Yes!" Tessa's eyes grew wide. "You, too?"

Chicky nodded. "Yup!"

They exchanged a little hug and shared a cab from there and the men followed along carrying bags and talking about Husker football.

* * *

Roberta began to regret her decision when she entered the enormous conference room at the Hilton. Everywhere she looked there were people who had to be better cooks than she was. Who did she think she was? Some kind of chef? Seriously. She was just a small town girl with a good potato salad recipe.

But, she'd come all this way, she might as well stay.

Roberta went to the registration table and picked up her cooking partners assignment. The names on the list looked interesting enough. The meal would be summer fare. Sausage-stuffed pepper appetizers, her potato salad, chili, and cookies.

The Competition Begins

The four girls found each other and sat down to visit. Gloria looked around the room as they chatted, waiting for the opening remarks. There were eighty great cooks here to try their hands at winning the grand prize of $40,000. They all milled around, finding their teammates, and talking about their recipes. Around the perimeter of the room, cooking cubicles were set up for each team. Gloria couldn't wait to get started. As she continued to scan the room, her eyes landed on a man behind a bar. He was quite attractive, dressed in a white shirt and black vest as he jostled up a cocktail in a metal shaker. She felt a little warm just watching him and then his eyes rose and locked with hers. Her breath caught in her throat. There was something so familiar about him, but she didn't think she'd ever seen him before. Nerves made her look away. Just in time. A woman was tapping on the mike at the front of the room.

"Ladies and gentlemen, my name is Sheila Nells and I'm here to welcome you to the First Annual, Hot in the Kitchen, Cooking Competition! And you know what they say when you can't take the heat?"

The crowd yelled out, "Get out of the kitchen!"

"That's right!"

Mrs. Nells talked for what seemed like an eternity. She droned on and on, introducing everyone who helped plan the event, and giving credit to an extensive list of sponsors.

"Now. I want to introduce the most important person here!"

The crowd looked around wondering who it could possibly be. Wolfgang Puck? Mario Batali? Emeril Lagasse? Warren Buffet?

"Ladies and gentlemen, allow me to introduce to you, our own mixologist, Hank James!"

Up onto the stage walked the handsome man Gloria had spied behind the bar. He took a graceful bow and gave the crowd a charming smile. The ladies in the audience couldn't resist the eye candy. A few hoots and whistles filled the air.

"Mr. James is the owner of the most talked about new cocktail club and restaurant in Omaha, *Inferno*. Hank will work with your team to create the perfect cocktail for your menu and he will also be available all day to make you as many drinks as you want throughout the competition…for free!"

The crowd burst into clapping and hoots.

Sheila Nells went on to explain the rules of the competition and how to proceed. By the time she gave contestants the go-ahead to get started, they were like horses busting out of the gate.

Gloria ran to claim a cooking cubicle and began chopping and dicing. Team members only had a half hour to prepare their course. The girls helped each other and chatted as, one by one, they created their specialties. The large conference room was filled with aromas and the sound of sizzling pans and knives chopping down onto cutting boards.

* * *

"All that's left is the drink," Roberta said, hoping she'd be delegated to go visit with the sexy mixologist, Hank James.

Gloria looked over toward the bar and shook her head. "Not me. He makes me nervous. I can't really explain why."

Tessa glanced out into the crowd to see Jacob sitting visiting with other husbands. She smiled. "I don't need the thrill. I've got my boy-toy right over there."

Chicky sat down on a folding chair behind their counter. "Not me. My dogs are barkin'. I need to rest."

Roberta's eyebrows danced and her face split in a grin. "Guess it's me, then!" She made her way over to the bar and stood in a line of women all prepared to flirt with Hank James.

"Hello, Roberta," Hank drawled with a southern accent dripping with honey.

"How do you know my name?" Roberta's eyes widened, her hand covering her mouth.

Hank leaned onto the bar and offered a sexy smile. "You have a nametag on." He winked.

Roberta blushed and giggled nervously. "Of course." Then she fanned herself. "My goodness. It's hot over here. All the air conditioning vents must be pointed at the stoves. You're in a real hot box over here!"

"Oh, I love the heat." Hank turned and grabbed a glass, plunked in some ice, and poured tea from a pitcher, then handed it to Roberta. "Here. This will cool you down. Now, tell me what your four-course meal is and I'll make something sinfully delicious just for you.

A few minutes later Roberta returned to her cooking partners and presented the Lynchburg Lemonade.

"Man is that bartender steamy." Roberta fanned herself. "I mean, not just sexy hot…hot, hot. She wiped the moisture beaded up on her brow. Gloria scowled.

* * *

Roberta's words struck a chord with Gloria. She inhaled sharply at the memory of another man who brought heat with his charisma. She shook her head. Gloria tried not to think about that night very often. "No man that sexy should ever be trusted." Gloria could see Roberta gaze in Hank's direction, oblivious to her warning. *Some girls have to learn from their own mistakes.*

* * *

Chicky was right. They won. Easily. The competition was fierce. The teams to either side of them were out for blood, it seemed. But the girls weren't concerned. They had fun, they cooked away and chattered, and truth be told, each one of them had been through far worse than a silly contest. In the end, the judges fawned over each and every course of the summer meal Gloria, Roberta, Chicky and Tessa presented. Oh. And every judge heartily enjoyed Hank's Lynchburg Lemonade. It seemed to seal the deal.

* * *

Dan knew his wife better than she knew herself. Once she set her mind to something, there was just no stopping her. From what he could tell, the other three girls on the team were equally determined. He wasn't surprised either when they took the $40,000 prize.

"Can I please have the winning team come to the stage," Sheila Nells announced at the mike.

The four women ran with lively steps to claim their enormous cardboard check.

"First a toast," Sheila announced as Hank James came forward with a tray loaded with champagne-filled glasses.

"Here's to four women with fire in their hearts. True cooks. True champions. They have proved they can take the heat. Here's to hoping they will all stay in the kitchen!"

Dan almost burst with pride as he clicked picture after picture with his new Nikon D7000. Gazing through the viewfinder, he went from proud to pissed. It seemed in every picture, Hank James had one of the four ladies on his arm. Mr. Sexy Mixologist was never very far away from Chicky and her winning team and it wasn't sitting right with Dan, not one bit at all. Hank didn't deserve to be part of their moment of glory. What the hell was he snuggling up to these gals for anyway? He'd had plenty of attention today. He didn't need to steal theirs.

Dan put the cap on the camera lens and went to get a breath of fresh air. He wandered through the large room as balloons floated and the confetti still drifted through the air. He ended up in the men's restroom and was at the urinal when the very person he was bothered about came to use the spot beside him. Dan glanced over. *Great.* Dan hoped he could keep his mouth shut and not give Hank a piece of his mind.

"Those are some hot little ladies who won the contest." Hank said, then whistled. "Even the pregnant redhead, I wouldn't kick out of bed for eating crackers."

Dan zipped his pants as heat crept up his neck and turned his face crimson. They were the only people in the restroom and Dan was considering feeding Mr. James a urinal cake. Dan was a good six inches taller and fifty pounds heavier than Hank, and beating the smirk off his face would have been fun. Dan's temper was sneaking up his collar and burning his neck, but calmer tactics were probably in order.

"That pregnant redhead is my wife." Dan cracked his knuckles and stared at Hank, assuming the man would apologize.

"I know." Hank said, then stared back at Dan with a smoldering glare dripping with arrogance. He turned to go wash his hands, then left the bathroom without another word.

Dan watched the door close behind Hank and felt utterly confused as to why he hadn't grabbed him by his scrawny neck and smashed his face into the tile wall. It was as though time stood still. Hank James was a man Dan planned to keep his eye on for the rest of the night. Dan left the bathroom to go find Chicky and her newfound friends…and to keep a close watch on Hank James.

* * *

Most of the contestants cleared out once they congratulated the winners and enjoyed a drink or two, but everyone on the winning team stayed around to relax and have the benefit of a few more laughs. The balloons were beginning to drift down from the ceiling and streamers littered the floor. The group of six, Gloria, Roberta, Chicky, Tessa, Jacob and Dan, sat around a large round table as they talked about what they each planned to do with their respective $10,000 share of the prize money. Besides them in the large room, only Hank, Sheila Nells, and a few hotel staff remained.

"Well, I have my heart set on a vacation to Jamaica. I want to float in an infinity pool and drink Mojitos while I read a juicy romance novel." Chicky beamed at Dan. "After the baby comes, of course."

"Sounds great to me. I know my mom can't wait to babysit." Dan responded, but he was distracted. He had no intention of letting Hank out of his sight and Dan couldn't help but notice how Hank seemed to hover close to their table, gifting the ladies with his suave smiles.

"We have a honeymoon to pay for. I'm thinking Hawaii." Tessa smiled at Jacob and he reached over and squeezed her hand.

* * *

Roberta also kept her eye on Hank. He was mesmerizing. He kept giving her little winks and she had a funny feeling she might be getting to know him better before the evening was done. At least she hoped. Normally, Roberta wasn't the type to flirt, but there was just something about this man. The longer she watched him, the more confident she felt. It was as though all of her synapses were firing. Ideas were dancing around her brain and she could hardly believe it herself when she said, "I've always wanted to go to culinary school."

Everyone turned to give her their full attention.

"Really?" Gloria smiled. "That's wonderful. How exciting!"

"I know. I didn't even realize how much I wanted to do that until just today. But it feels like I've *always* wanted to and maybe I just realized it. Weird."

Roberta felt energized, like the world was her oyster, and all she had to do was reach out and grab whatever she wanted.

"You absolutely *can* do anything you put your mind to." Hanks words melted like butter in Roberta's ears. He had walked up behind her and set a Tom Collins in front of her.

* * *

Everyone shifted their attention to Hank. Dan glared at him like an intruder. An odd feeling came over Gloria. She sat quietly, lost in her own thoughts, or a memory of a feeling she had once.

"So, Gloria. What will you do with your share?" Chicky switched the focus back to the girls as she propped her swelled feet up on a chair.

"Yeah," Tessa chimed in. "What is your heart set on, Gloria?"

"You'll all laugh at me." Gloria confessed as she hung her head. She couldn't believe she was considering saying out loud the thoughts now pulsating through her mind.

"We wouldn't," Roberta assured her new friend. "Hey, I admitted I wanted to go to culinary school."

"I'll bet I know what Gloria wants to do with her money." Hank set down a fresh Cosmo in front of her.

Gloria's face flushed. She was interested in what his guess would be so she looked at him with raised eyebrows, inviting his speculation.

"Gloria wants to open a restaurant." He put his hand on her shoulder and something in her recognized a familiar sensation. It was as though his touch brought a jolt to her consciousness. She felt absolutely positive she wanted to embrace this new course in life.

"I *do* want to open a restaurant. How did you know that?" Gloria turned and stared deep into Hank's sultry eyes, her eyebrows knitted in disbelief.

"Oh, I suspect about a fourth of the people competing here today have that same dream. You're one of four competitors here at this table so the odds were in his favor." Dan piped up. He stood and adjusted his belt as he stared at Hank.

Hank smiled at Dan and set a Piña Colada in front of Tessa as he placed his hand on *her* shoulder…"Is this what you were drinking?" Tessa nodded, then tilted her head as she looked over at Gloria.

"You know, I have to admit, I've toyed with the idea myself," Tessa confessed, although she also looked shocked at her own idea. Jacob looked at his fiancée with an awestruck expression.

"Really?" Gloria leaned forward, intrigued and delighted she wasn't the only one.

Roberta's face seemed to reach an epiphany. "You know, Gloria. I'd like more information about what you're thinking. My job isn't going to take me anywhere. A new adventure might be just what I need. You need someone who can make potato salad? I can cook other things, too. And if I do go to culinary school, I could be a real asset."

"Wow. This is like a dream coming true." Gloria couldn't believe her dream might have a chance of at least serious discussion.

Hank made his way over to Chicky, but before he got that far, Dan took the cola from Hank's hand. "I'll take care of my redhead. Thanks anyway." Dan laid his heavy hand on Hank's shoulder and the look in Dan's eyes said he wasn't fooling.

Hank smiled. "You know, ladies, as Sheila said, I own a new cocktail club and restaurant right here in Omaha, Inferno. I'm always looking for fresh blood." His gaze floated between Tessa, Gloria, and Roberta. "I'd be willing to take you girls under my wing, so to speak. You have all proved today you have what it takes to be winners. I could really see working with all of you. You ladies would add just the right amount of spice to my kitchen." His confidence was overwhelming. Those enticing words. Who could resist his charming offer?

The girl's faces lit up and they began to chatter and buzz with questions.

Dan watched for a while then had enough. Who in the hell did this Hank James think he was and how in the hell did he manage to wrap every woman, except Chicky, around his finger so quickly?

"Now settle down girls. What's gotten into you women?" Dan stood and his voice broke their chatter. "I run a bar and restaurant, too, you know. It's a hell of a lot of work. Are you girls sure you're up to this big of an adventure?" Dan went over to stand by Hank. He towered over him and glared at Hank. Dan wasn't about to let his slick good looks and smooth talk lead these nice women into something they couldn't handle.

"I know how to work hard." Gloria nodded enthusiastically.

"Hard work is my middle name," Roberta added.

Tessa drummed her fingers on the table and looked at Jacob. "What do you think?"

"I can't tell you what to do, honey. But I will tell you I'll be in your corner no matter what you decide." Tessa beamed at her man. "I'd guess I'd be willing to keep talking about it at least."

"I have to admit. It's a tough business, but we enjoy it." Chicky looked over at Dan with eyes filled with pride.

"It *is* a fine business to be in, and that's why we've been talking about expanding. I think if you girls are truly interested, I would like you to consider coming down to work with us." Dan stepped in front of Hank and gave him a distrustful stare. "I'm very fair. We have a loyal clientele. And I'd be honest with you all." Dan's eyes shot bullets at Hank. "If any of you want to come partner up and help me expand, I'd be all ears. We have the know-how and keep our customers happy. And you…" Dan pointed at Hank. "I don't trust you any further than I can see you. You keep your distance from my girl. And, I'm sorry, ladies…I am going to warn you away from his smooth lines and big promises. I do not think his intentions are honorable."

Chicky crossed her arms over her chest and so did Jacob, but they both grinned at Dan's commanding presence. Tessa blushed when she saw Jacob's reaction. Roberta covered her mouth and giggled, and Gloria gave Dan a thankful nod.

Hank backed away and lifted his palms to the ceiling.

"You can't blame me for trying," he offered but Dan kept his eyes locked on him until he finally backed out of the room.

Gloria felt coolness come over her and she sighed. She *really* needed to find a nice man. She was too easily influenced. Dan was right. Hank was pushing for something he shouldn't have had anything to do with.

"You know what, Dan? I think I *am* going to come down to visit you at your place and see what I think. How's that sound?"

"Sounds good to me. Come any time." Dan grinned.

"Can I catch a ride with you?" Roberta asked Gloria.

"Of course." Gloria nodded.

"The more the merrier." Chicky laughed.

"So how 'bout you?" Jacob asked Tessa.

Tessa paused and stared at Jacob. Jacob shrugged. "You have to make that decision on your own."

"No, girls. It's not for me. I have a life I love in St. Louis. But I expect you all to keep me posted on your progress."

Jacob wiped fake sweat from his brow and everyone chuckled.

Dan nodded, then sat down to nurse his beer. As the ladies visited, he fell completely in love with the idea of these adorable gals helping him run The GiddyUp. To hell with Hank James, Dan thought. These women could take the heat, and had the strength to build a great future. Together, they all could accomplish anything. He could just feel it. This idea was a recipe for success.

LYNCHBURG LEMONADE

1 cup ice cubes
1 (1.5 fluid ounce) jigger Tennessee whiskey
1 (1.5 fluid ounce) jigger sweet and sour mix
1 (1.5 fluid ounce) jigger triple sec
3/4 cup chilled lemon-lime soda

Pour over ice and stir.
Serve with a slice each of orange and lemon.

Cheers!

Author G. M. Barlean is a Nebraska girl, married to a farmer, mother of two adult children, and a woman who loves to cook.

Website:
GMBarlean.com

Blogsite:
Gmbarlean.wordpress.com

Special thanks to those who provided recipes:
Sausage Stuffed Peppers: Miriam Ostermeier
Chocolate Chip Krispy Cookies:
Karna Ostermeier Ahlschwede

The chili and potato salad recipes are
the author's own creation.

Made in the USA
Charleston, SC
05 January 2016